ALWAYS IN MY HEART

SAMANTHA HICKS

ALWAYS IN MY HEART

SAMANTHA HICKS

Affinity
Rainbow Publications

2020

Always in My Heart
© 2020 by Samantha Hicks

Affinity E-Book Press NZ LTD
Canterbury, New Zealand

1st Edition

ISBN: 978-1-98-858881-0

Editor: CK King
Proof Editor: Alexis Smith
Cover Design: Irish Dragon Design
Production Design: Affinity Publication Services

ACKNOWLEDGMENTS

Writing is a very solitary process. I spend hours every week crafting characters and finding ways of bringing about a happy ever after. Whilst doing this, the publishing process doesn't come to mind often. It's not until submission, editing, cover design, and proofreading takes place that the creating of a 'book' gets my excitement building for the eventual release date. The joy of holding a copy of something I have spent months creating never gets old. But of course, it's not just me involved. I am eternally grateful Affinity continues to work with me. To help make my jumbled manuscript into something you readers can enjoy. The work Affinity put into helping us authors is amazing. Julie, Mel, and Nancy are a wonderful team and I couldn't ask for nicer people to accompany me on my writing journey. CK did an outstanding job in editing. I have learned a lot from her skills and have no doubt the writing in my next book will benefit from her efforts.

As usual my thanks go to my friends and family. Without their love, support, and encouragement, my dream of being an author may not have come true. My biggest thank you goes to Finley, my springer spaniel. Tapping away on my keyboard is less lonely with you by my side.

Also, a special mention to Hannah, my friend and neighbour. Thank you for all the times you play with Finn and our chats.

TABLE OF CONTENTS

PROLOGUE

Gabriella Carter stepped through the patio door and bounded down the steps and through the garden. She stopped by the concrete wall that surrounded the property. She checked her watch, nearly ten thirty at night. She was tired and tipsy. All she wanted was to go home. Nicole Turner had invited her to this party, and Gabby hadn't known how to say no. She was more of a homebody, preferring to watch movies than be out all night. But Nicole had insisted. They had met a few weeks ago at the supermarket. Gabby found her attractive and interesting, and didn't hesitate to give Nicole her phone number. They had texted ever since. This was their first proper date, not the kind of date Gabby would have preferred, but it would have to do.

Nicole was still inside, chatting to one of her friends. Hazel. An involuntary smile came to Gabby's lips, as she remembered their introduction. Haze was cute, short blonde hair and stunning blue eyes. Gabby's breath had left her when they shook hands. There was something about the feel of that contact that made tiny sparks zip across her skin. Gabby sighed. She was here with Nicole. *We're not technically girlfriends, but I shouldn't be out here thinking about someone else.*

Gabby tilted her head back to look at the sky, the moon just visible behind the clouds. The chill air did wonders to cool her overheated skin. She took another deep breath, then turned to head back inside. Haze was striding toward her, her intense gaze zeroed in on Gabby.

"Haze, hi."

There was no verbal response. Haze put one hand on Gabby's waist, the other on her cheek, and pulled her forward. Gabby didn't have a chance to react, as Haze's mouth crashed onto hers. Momentarily stunned, Gabby didn't move, just allowed Haze to kiss her. Need gave way and Gabby kissed her back. She grabbed Haze's hips and pulled her closer still. The feel of Haze's tongue duelling with her own sent a flood of arousal straight to her lace underwear. She had never been kissed like this before, with such passion and urgency. Gabby wasn't sure how long they'd kissed before Haze's mouth stilled and left Gabby's.

"What's wrong?" Gabby asked, her breath coming in quick gasps.

"We can't do this."

"Why not?"

Haze stepped back and ran a hand through her hair, then over her mouth. "You're here with Nikki."

"This is our first date. Hardly going out with each other." Gabby took a step forward to resume the kissing. The feel of Haze would forever be imprinted on her skin, and she needed more.

"No. It's wrong. She really likes you."

"Then why did you kiss me?"

Haze shrugged. "I'm drunk."

"Bullshit." No one who was drunk could kiss like that. "Haze, it's okay."

"No. I'm sorry. I have to go."

Haze turned and sprinted away. Gabby soon lost sight of her in the crowd by the patio door. She slumped back against the wall, her fingers tracing her swollen lips. She had never been kissed so thoroughly. She was attracted to Haze, no doubt about that. *I hope I get another chance to see her.* She wasn't going to let this opportunity get away from her.

"Hey, babe," Nicole said from beside her. Gabby hadn't heard her arrive. "What are you doing out here?"

"Just getting some air."

"You look a little flushed. Are you sick?"

No, just incredibly turned on. "Too much beer, I think."

"Let's go then. Don't want you puking."

Gabby allowed Nicole to take her hand and lead her through the garden and house, then out the front door. Gabby couldn't help but look for Haze in the throngs of people, disappointed when she didn't see her. *I guess I'll see her another time.*

3

CHAPTER ONE

"I promise, I'll be back before the meeting starts." A bluetooth earpiece captured Gabby Turner's voice, as she sped along the motorway toward her home on the outskirts of Bristol. "I have to give the assignments back today, so the kids can work on them over the weekend." She glanced at the dashboard, noting the time on the digital clock. Gabby had taught maths at the local high school for the last five years, a job she loved. Yes, the thirteen-year-olds could sometimes get rowdy and refuse to listen, but mostly they were a good bunch. She enjoyed helping them learn something new. There was nothing better than seeing the pride in a child's face when they finally grasped the equation they were learning. She was due back at the school in thirty minutes for a staff meeting she couldn't be late for. It would be one of those meetings where nothing was really said, but the headteacher would drone on for ages about attendances and school spirit and the like. Nothing important, but Gabby knew the head would go crazy if she wasn't there. Edith Drake was a stickler for the rules. As much as her strict attitude frustrated the staff, Gabby was glad for her leadership. Their school was the highest ranked in the district and the most sought after come enrolment time. Edith had brought the school up to that level and Gabby wouldn't want it any other way.

"I think Edie wants to ask you to be in charge of tickets sales for the end-of-year play," Sharon said. "You have to be there."

"I will. I'm on my street now. It won't take me two minutes to grab the folder." Gabby disconnected the call and threw the earpiece onto the passenger seat. She pulled up to the terraced, two-bedroom home she shared with Nicole, frowning at an unfamiliar car. She thought, for a moment, a neighbour might have parked in their driveway due to the lack of parking on the narrow street. Glancing up ahead, Gabby dismissed the idea; the street was practically empty at two thirty in the afternoon.

She got out of the car and peeked through the window of the strange vehicle, not seeing anything of note. A moment of panic surged through her as she looked at her front door. Is this a break in? Are they inside robbing me? Not likely. Gabby and Nicole lived in a modest neighbourhood. Everyone knew their neighbours. The virtually nonexistent crime rate was what sold Gabby on the house in the first place. She wanted somewhere safe to raise a family. This part of Bristol was ideal.

5

Feeling foolish, she walked up the pathway and unlocked her front door. Nicole's grey, wool coat hung on the coatrack. She had worn it to work that morning and wasn't due home until seven that evening. Gabby closed the door quietly, her heart pounding against her ribs. She heard movement from upstairs. The sound of laughter wafted down, and Gabby instantly knew Nicole was there. What startled Gabby was that Nicole wasn't alone. Another female voice giggled.

"Get over here with that and fuck me till I come."

Gabby's hand flew to her mouth to stop the sob from leaving her throat. Her other hand rested against the wall, helping to keep her upright.

"You asked for it, baby," Nicole replied, her voice husky and dripping in sensuality.

Gabby had heard that voice many times, and it left no doubt in her mind as to what was going on in her bedroom. Gabby slowly made her way upstairs, avoiding the floorboards she knew would creak. Halfway up the stairs, Gabby peeked over the landing into their bedroom. There, stood at the foot of the bed, Nicole was screwing a younger woman who looked to be about twenty-five. Gabby blinked, trying to make the visual disappear, hoping it was a dream. No, it was real.

Nicole was cheating on her.

She carefully made her way down the stairs, her hand going to her stomach. She felt sick, but that wasn't why her hand went there. The baby had kicked, a common occurrence recently. Gabby had joked that she was brewing a footballer intent on kicking around her internal organs for fun. She was five months pregnant with her first child, one that she and

6

Nicole had planned for years. Nicole had wanted the baby just as much as Gabby did.

How could she cheat on me?

Gabby got out of the house and into her car, pulling away faster than what was considered safe. She stopped a few streets away. Her hands went to her face as she sobbed, her shoulders shaking. How could Nicole do this to her? They had been married for eight years, known each other for ten. They were happy, in love, hardly ever arguing. How was it possible she hadn't realised Nicole was cheating on her?

How long has it been going on?

She sat there for a long while, her head spinning with the betrayal she felt. She knew she should have confronted Nicole. *I should have stormed up the stairs and slapped her.* That wasn't Gabby's style. She was kind, gentle, and loving. She didn't do violence, and she was never any good at confrontation. She started the car again and drove to the only person who would have any idea what was going on. Hazel Evens was Nicole's best friend.

Gabby paid no mind to the homework she should have collected and the staff meeting she would now miss.

†

The pounding on her front door startled Haze. Rubbing her eyes to clear them of the last of her sleep, she righted herself on the couch and ran a hand through her short, blonde hair. The pounding came again. "Alright, alright, I'm coming." She stumbled through the living room to the front door and opened it wide. "Gabby? What are you doing here?" It wasn't unusual for Gabby or Nicole to just pop over unannounced, but it was very rare for Gabby to show up in the middle of a school day. Haze worked from home as a web designer and rarely left the house, unless she had a client meeting or mundane errands. Those she put off until she absolutely had to do them. No one visited Haze during the workday, which was fine with her. Haze preferred to work late into the night and catch up on sleep during the day.

"Is there anything you want to tell me about Nicole?" Gabby demanded, her tone tinged with anger, her gaze so piercing, Haze thought she could feel it blasting through her skin. She studied Gabby's bloodshot eyes. Her gorgeous, chestnut curls were a mess, and her lips were set in a thin line. Haze had never seen her look so lost and fuming. *Whatever Nikki has done, it's bad.* She shook her head, confused over what was going on.

"What are you talking about? I haven't seen Nikki in weeks." This was true. They were best friends, had been since they were four years old, but their schedules tended to clash. Arranging time to get together was hard. Besides that, seeing them so happy and in love wore thin on Haze's nerves. Perpetually single, Haze was sick of being the third wheel.

"Please, Haze. I need to know if you knew. Please don't lie to me."

Haze reached for Gabby's hand when she saw a tremor steal through her body. She pulled Gabby into the lounge and out of the cold. "Gabby, you're scaring me. What's happened?"

Gabby stood in the middle of the lounge, wrapping her arms around her growing bump. Haze's gaze followed the movement, cursing the fact that Nikki had met Gabby first and it was Nikki's baby in there, not hers. Haze had been in love with Gabby since the moment she laid eyes on her at that stupid party. Those dark eyes had pulled her in and hadn't let go in the ten years since. It was the classic cliché, in love with your best friend's wife. She had worked hard to put those feelings aside, over the years, but they still lingered. Haze was happy for Nikki and Gabby. They had found true love and were making a family together. Seeing Gabby on the verge of crying and so distraught confused the hell out of Haze. In all the years they had been together, Haze had never seen them cross words, even once.

"I just went home to pick up some schoolwork, and I saw Nicole screwing the brains out of some young slut."

Those words released the tears. Haze stepped forward and took Gabby in her arms, holding Gabby's head in the crook of her neck. Shaky arms around her waist returned the embrace. Gabby squeezed tight as she cried.

She must be mistaken. There's no way Nikki would ever cheat on her. Haze had known Nikki for thirty years. In all that time, she had never been one to play around. Nikki had always dreamed of having her own family one day. She didn't date much. Knowing what it was she wanted in a woman, she didn't feel the need to go out with someone she knew she wouldn't have a future with. When Nikki met Gabby, things had clicked straight away. Nikki loved her. *No, there's no way she'd cheat on her.*

"Are you sure?" Haze instantly regretted her words. Gabby shoved her away, hard, causing Haze to stumble over her trainers. She landed on the couch she had been napping on not ten minutes before. Haze didn't need to hear the answer. The fire in Gabby's glare told her she was crazy to even think she would make this up.

"I came home, walked up the stairs, and saw them. Of course I'm sure." Gabby took a breath and sat next to Haze, resting her head on the back of the couch. "I can't believe this. We're about to have a baby." She turned her head to look at Haze, her eyes wounded. "How could she do this to me?"

Haze lifted her arm and settled it around Gabby's shoulder, pulling her close. The scent of her coconut shampoo caused her to falter a moment before replying. Gabby always had this effect on her. It always took Haze a second to centre herself and remember Gabby was off-limits. "I swear I didn't know. I want to kick her ass for doing this to you."

"I can't go back there. Not now I know what's she's been doing in our bed." Her hand settled on her bump, rubbing back and forth. "I'm questioning everything she ever said to me, all her late-night meetings, having to stay over at hotels because conferences ran over and it was too late to drive. Was she cheating on me then? Fucking women while I was at home feeling sorry for her because she had to work so late?"

"Don't do this to yourself. You'll make yourself sick." Haze rested her hand on top of Gabby's where it still lay on her bump. "You need to think about this little one. Second-guessing everything will stress you out. You need to talk to her—"

"I can't. I don't want to see her."

"I know you don't, but you need to find out the truth instead of worrying over it."

Gabby didn't answer for a long moment. She stared at her stomach, her hand grasping Haze's. "Can I stay here? Just until I can find somewhere more permanent?"

Haze knew she shouldn't get in the middle of this. Whatever trouble Gabby and Nikki were getting into was none of her business. But Gabby was her friend too. Haze couldn't condone what Nikki had been doing, and would let her know that. *Right now, Gabby is my concern.* Gabby's eyes were hopeful as she gazed at her. Haze found herself agreeing without hesitation. She would do anything for Gabby.

"You know you can stay here for as long as you want. I'll get the airbed out and set it up in here. You can take my room."

"Oh no, Haze. I'm not taking your room from you. I'll be fine out here."

"No. You're pregnant, and you need a proper bed. I've slept in worse places."

Gabby stared at her for a moment, then nodded. "Okay. Would you mind if I laid down now? I'm exhausted after all this and just want to rest for a while."

"Of course. Come on." Haze stood and helped Gabby from the couch. She led her down the hallway. "I'll just change the sheets."

"This is fine, you're the cleanest person I know."

That was true, being at home all day allowed Haze the time to keep her two-bedroom apartment spotless. Cleaning was a good way of destressing and helped clear her mind when she was stuck on a particular design she couldn't get right.

"All right." Haze closed the blinds and pulled back the duvet, while Gabby kicked off her shoes and removed her jumper, leaving her in just a tight T-shirt and her trousers. She slipped into bed and pulled the duvet over herself. Haze made her way to the door. "I'll be in the office if you need anything."

"Actually, do you mind staying a while? I don't want to be alone."

Haze only hesitated a second before settling on the bed, back up against the headboard. Gabby rolled over and flung her arm around Haze's waist, her head settling on her jean covered thigh.

"Thank you."

"No problem."

As Gabby drifted off, Haze's thoughts turned to Nikki. She couldn't reconcile the woman she knew and loved like a sister to the cheater she so obviously was. *How did I miss it?* Casting her mind back over the years, not once could she think of a time when Nikki had lied to her. Nikki had never seemed distant or as though she were hiding something. She must have done this sort of thing before. The odds of getting caught the first time were rather slim. To be so brazen as to have an affair in your own home took guts and planning. Someone starting an affair wouldn't do that, would they? Haze couldn't come up with any answers. Her loyalty to Nikki was dwindling. She looked down at Gabby, softly snoring next to her. Yes, her loyalty to Nikki had vanished the moment Gabby told her what she saw. Haze's only concern was for Gabby and her unborn baby. Whatever excuse Nikki came up with wouldn't ever be good enough to do this to someone as sweet and loving as Gabby. Only a fool would betray her like that. Gabby was precious, the most honourable and caring woman Haze had ever known. Again, she cursed the fact Nikki had met her first. Haze would never have done what Nikki did to her.

Without meaning to, Haze's eyes drifted shut. Soon, she too fell asleep.

CHAPTER TWO

For the second time that day, Haze was awoken by the sound of pounding on her door. She opened her eyes, as Gabby stirred next to her. The bedroom was cast in shadow, a clue to the late hour. She rubbed her eyes, then disentangled herself from Gabby. The pounding came again.

"Haze, open up," Nikki shouted from outside the front door.

Haze immediately felt guilty for lying in bed with Gabby, no matter how innocent it had been. It wasn't the first time they had shared a bed. Many times over the years, they had all slept at each other's houses, sometimes crashing out on couches or the floor. This felt different somehow. Knowing Nikki was cheating on Gabby, and that Gabby had turned to Haze for comfort, opened a tiny door in Haze's heart. She should slam that door shut right away. Gabby was, and always would be, off-limits. These were her best friends. She wouldn't come between them, no matter how much she wanted Gabby for herself.

Haze shot from the bed and righted her T-shirt. "How did she know you were here?"

Gabby sat up, running her hand through her curls and shrugged. "There are a limited number of places I would go." Her eyes dimmed a little. "I don't want to see her."

"I'll sort it, don't worry." Haze smiled quickly, then strode from the room. She reached the door just as Nikki knocked again.

"Haze, thank God."

It wasn't hard to miss the look of panic in her gaze. Her cheeks were flushed, and her body trembled with her urgency. For a moment, Haze thought maybe she should have contacted Nikki the minute Gabby turned up, then she remembered why Gabby was there. The feeling of guilt fled.

"Is Gabby all right? I've been ringing her mobile and searching for her for hours. The school called and told me she hadn't returned to work." She pushed past Haze, her gaze roaming the open-plan living room and kitchen.

"She doesn't want to see you." Haze folded her arms across her chest, trying desperately to control the urge to hit Nikki. Never, in all the years of their friendship, had she ever wanted to do that. Her anger was on the brink of exploding. Nikki turned to face her.

"What? Why?"

Movement from the hallway caught Haze's attention. Gabby padded along the carpet in her socks.

"You damn well know why," Gabby seethed.

Haze walked around Nicole and stood by Gabby, wanting to be close to her to show her support.

"I have no idea what you're talking about. I've been worried sick." Nicole took a step forward, but Gabby stopped her with her hand in the air, palm facing forward.

"I saw you screwing some woman on our bed."

Nicole shook her head. "What? Honey, that's crazy. I've been at work all day."

"I came home to pick up a folder and saw you two fucking like you were in a porno."

For a moment Nicole's eyes went wide. Fear flashed across her features before she schooled her expression. "That's ridiculous." She glanced at Haze. "You don't believe this, do you?" Without waiting for Haze to respond, she said to Gabby, "Honey, you're pregnant, perhaps your hormones are making you see things that aren't real."

"How dare you insult my intelligence," Gabby shouted. "I know what I saw. Ow." Gabby's hand went to her stomach as she bent at the waist.

"Are you okay?" Haze reached out to steady her.

"Get your hands off my wife."

Gabby righted herself and pointed at Nicole. "No, you don't get to tell her what to do. This is her house, and you're in the wrong. Get out."

"I don't believe this. If anyone should be worried about affairs, it's me. What are you doing here anyway, and in Haze's bedroom? Perhaps you two are the ones who are fucking."

Haze was amazed at how calm her own voice came out. "How dare you!" Nikki knew she would never cross that line. For her to suggest it was a slap in the face Haze didn't deserve. Nikki was only trying to deflect the attention from herself for being caught out, but the barb stung, nonetheless.

"Oh come on. We all know you've had the hots for her for years."

"You need to leave before this gets out of hand." Haze wasn't sure how much longer she could remain civil. Nikki was her best friend, and she didn't want to ruin that over dumb accusations. She needed to find out what was going on with her before she did anything rash, like cut her out of her life for good. Everyone made mistakes. Haze hoped Nikki had only made the one and hadn't been cheating on Gabby for a long time. For some reason, that betrayal would hurt more than just one foolish sex session. It shouldn't matter how many times someone cheated, once was enough, but Haze needed to know the truth; and so did Gabby.

"Fine, I'll go. I'll give you some time to think about what you think you saw."

"I don't need time," Gabby said quietly, her eyes tearing. "I'll be by at ten o'clock tomorrow morning to collect some things. Don't be there when I arrive."

"This is ridiculous. Call me when you've come to your senses."

Nikki said no more. She turned on her heel and slammed the front door behind her. Haze briefly closed her eyes, thinking what a God awful mess this all was. She turned to look at Gabby, who stood in the living room with tears rolling freely down her cheeks.

"How can she stand there and deny it? Blaming it on my hormones, for God's sake."

Haze didn't think as she crossed over to Gabby and pulled her into a tight hug. "She obviously didn't expect to be seen by you. She was caught off guard and has gone into defensive mode."

"Well, I know what I saw," Gabby mumbled into Haze's chest. Pulling back, she asked, "Have you got anything to eat? I'm starving."

"Yeah, come on." Haze led them into the kitchen. She guided Gabby onto a chair, then set about making ham sandwiches for them both. As she worked, thoughts of what Nikki had said raced through her mind. *It's true that I love Gabby more than I should.* Nikki figured that out rather quickly, years ago. They had even discussed it, once over a few beers. Haze made it perfectly clear she would never act on those feelings, and Nikki believed her. To bring it up now is stirring shit that didn't need to be mentioned.

With her back to Gabby, she said, "Um, Gabby? About what Nikki said, you know, about me?" She glanced over her shoulder at her. "You know I would never do–"

"Haze, it's fine. You're the most honourable person I know. You'd never hurt anyone, even at your own expense."

Haze slid a plate onto the table in front of Gabby and sat down opposite her. "What do you mean?"

"I'm talking about before Nikki and I got together, officially, when you kissed me. I saw the interest in your eyes, but you backed away because you knew Nikki liked me. You didn't pursue me, because you knew it would upset her. That's what I'm talking about." She took a bite of her sandwich.

"We never spoke about that. I kinda thought you'd forgot." Haze couldn't look at Gabby, her embarrassment overwhelming her. She remembered that night at the party, just over ten years ago. Nicole and Gabby were "just friends" then. Knowing Nikki liked Gabby hadn't stopped Haze from catching up to her outside where she was cooling off. Haze had walked straight up to her and kissed her without warning. That moment had been the single hottest thing Haze had ever experienced, even more so than some of the sex she'd had with girlfriends. Tasting Gabby had been exquisite. When Gabby grabbed her and fiercely kissed her back, Haze thought she would come then and there. Nikki had come out looking for them. Haze ran away, embarrassed and ashamed that she had tried it on with her best friend's girl. She didn't see either of them for a month after that. When she did, Gabby and Nicole were officially dating. The realisation had shattered Haze's heart, and she tried desperately to get Gabby out of her mind. It didn't work, seeing her all the time, watching them plan the wedding, moving in together, and now the pregnancy. All of it cracked her heart a little bit more each time. Haze feared she would never get over her stupid feelings.

She hadn't told Gabby about having a crush on her but assumed Nikki had. It wouldn't surprise Haze if they'd had a good laugh about it. She chanced a look in Gabby's direction. She didn't see the mocking smile she expected, just kind eyes slightly hooded and staring intently at her. From any other woman, Haze would recognise the look as interest. This was Gabby and the way she always looked when they talked about anything serious.

"How could I forget a kiss that made my toes curl?" Gabby grinned.

Heat rushed to Haze's skin. She cleared her throat. Okay, so maybe there was a little teasing, but not in an unpleasant way. "You never said anything."

"It didn't matter. You backed away, and I fell in love with Nicole. No point talking about something that never should have happened in the first place."

Haze reached across the table, grasping Gabby's hand. "I'm your friend, Gabby. I'd never come between you two."

Gabby smiled quickly and shrugged. "I'm not sure there is an us anymore. Besides, I don't feel that way about you anyway. I'm sorry."

Gabby let go of her hand and took another bite of her sandwich, her gaze focused on the table. There was something in her demeanour that pinged Haze's antennae. Something told her Gabby didn't mean what she had just said, but Haze had to let it go. Too much was going on. All of their emotions were riding high. Any hopes Haze had of being with Gabby one day were just that, hopes. Gabby was with Nikki. No doubt they would sort their problems out and go on to live a happy life together as a family. Haze would do what she always had, be their friend, stay out of the way, and play the what-if game forever in her mind.

"Hey, I know that. Any naughty thoughts I had about you left years ago." The slight joke broke the tension. Gabby laughed then nodded, as if that was what she had hoped Haze would say. Haze would never make a move on her, and she wanted Gabby to believe that.

"Thanks, Haze."

"No problem."

CHAPTER THREE

Gabby groaned as she opened her eyes the following morning, wishing she could sleep longer. After the showdown with Nicole and the conversation with Haze, her night was filled with broken sleep and dreams of that powerful kiss from a younger Haze. God, that kiss felt great. If Haze had asked, I would have gone home with her. No doubt, the sex between us would have been amazing. Haze had backed away and they didn't see her for weeks. In that time, Gabby's attraction to Nicole grew stronger, and they fell in love. She had been happy in the last ten years, knowing she had made the right decision. Nicole was attentive and loving, doing everything she could for Gabby. She couldn't ask for a better partner. So when did it all go wrong? How could somebody as sweet as Nicole turn into a cheater? Gabby knew she would need to talk to her at some point, but she wasn't ready for that yet. Her heart was too decimated to fathom speaking with her rationally.

She climbed from the bed. After a quick stop in the bathroom, she went in search of Haze, finding her stretched out on the couch. They had tried to put up the airbed the previous evening, but it wouldn't inflate. Haze insisted the couch was fine. Looking at her, Gabby didn't think she looked comfortable in the least. Her feet hung off the end, and her head was at an unnatural angle, squashed between the armrest and cushion. She still looks as sexy as ever. Gabby smiled, as her gaze travelled over her strong body, covered only by a small blanket draped over her legs. Her chest and shoulders were bare. A light-blue tank top covered her small breasts. Haze's blonde hair was as dishevelled in sleep as it was during the day. For someone who didn't really care about her appearance, she did a good job of pulling off brooding and sensual. Whoever ended up with Haze would be in for a treat. Kind and compassionate, lean and sexy, funny and vulnerable, Haze was the whole package. Not for the first time, Gabby wondered what would have happened if Nicole hadn't come looking for them that night. Not that it mattered, Gabby loved her wife. She sighed, just as Haze opened her eyes and blinked at her, not yet fully awake.

"Good morning." Heat rose on Gabby's cheeks for the direction her thoughts had travelled. She hoped Haze didn't notice.

"Hey. Did you sleep okay?" Haze swung her legs off the couch and tossed the blanket onto the floor, making room for Gabby to sit down.

"Tossed and turned a lot. It's strange sleeping on my own. And this little one thought it would be fun to sit on my bladder all night long."

"I heard you moving around, but didn't want to disturb you."

"Sorry if I woke you." She glanced at Haze, then to the carpet, hating that her pulse raced at the concern in those blue eyes. Haze's eyes were her best feature. Gabby could always read them. That's how she knew Haze had feelings for her all these years, well, that and the kiss. No one could kiss like that and not have feelings behind it. At the beginning, knowing Haze liked her made her uncomfortable. Over time, it got easier. Haze had never done anything to pursue her, and for that Gabby was grateful. As much as she liked Haze, it was Nicole she loved. Well, up until yesterday when her world fell apart. "You shouldn't have to deal with all my drama."

"I told you, you're welcome here as long as you like. It'll be nice to have the company."

"Well if I get in the way, just tell me."

"I will." Haze glanced at the clock on the mantle, an heirloom from her gran. "When are you going to collect your things?"

"In about thirty minutes." Walking into the room where she'd caught Nicole having sex was not something Gabby was looking forward to. The thought filled her with a hate so strong she didn't know she could possess for the woman she loved.

"I'll make breakfast before you go."

Haze stood, but Gabby stopped her by grabbing her wrist, her skin cool to the touch. When did I start noticing the feel of her skin? "Not for me, thanks. I don't think my stomach can handle food right now."

"Tea?" Haze asked, raising her eyebrows.

"Please, thank you." She let her go and closed her eyes. One thing Nicole was right about, pregnancy hormones were playing tricks on her. Haze was her friend, nothing more. Just because Nicole was cheating on her, didn't mean Gabby should start noticing Haze's soft skin or the grey flecks in her irises, or how cute she looked when she slept. But she did, and it confused her. *Have those thoughts been there all along? Are they coming to the surface now, because of Nicole's actions?* Gabby didn't know, and she didn't want to find out. She stood and followed Haze into the kitchen. "What are you working on at the moment?"

"I've got a couple of projects going on." Haze poured hot water into two mugs. "One is a local barber, wanting to revamp their current website. The other is for a new dog walking service. They have no idea what they want, so they have given me free rein. I've mocked up a couple of ideas for them to pick from."

"Sounds interesting."

Haze grinned. "Sounds boring, but it pays the bills." She passed Gabby a mug and the sugar bowl.

"Nonsense. You're really talented." Gabby laughed when Haze's cheeks turned pink. She never really was any good at taking compliments. "And cute when you blush."

"Thanks."

They sipped their tea in silence for a few minutes. Gabby couldn't put off the inevitable any longer. "I best get going." She stood from the table and took her mug to the sink. Turning around, she asked, "I don't suppose you want to come with me?"

"Of course, no problem."

Gabby smiled her thanks, then tilted her head. "You say that a lot, you know." At Haze's raised eyebrows, she clarified, "No problem."

"That's because, for you, it really is no problem." She softened her features. "I know how difficult it'll be to go back there. I'm here for you all the way."

"Thanks, Haze."

Haze grinned. "No problem."

†

Twenty minutes later, Gabby pulled up to her own house, pleased when she didn't see Nicole's car. She briefly wondered if Nicole had spent the night at her girlfriend's house but quickly let the depressing thought go. It wouldn't do her any good to think about that.

"Do you want me to go in for you?" Haze drew Gabby's attention away from staring at the front door.

"No, it's okay. I need to do this. I just need to collect some clothes and toiletries." She looked back at the house. "I'm glad she isn't here. I don't think I could handle another argument, not yet anyway." She would need to see her eventually, but not until she had a chance to calm her anger. She wouldn't be able to get an explanation if Nicole was dead. *That's how I feel right now, like I could kill her.*

"Come on, let's get this over with."

Gabby nodded, then took a breath and opened the car door. She couldn't help but replay the scene in her mind. Her hand shook, as she tried to unlock the front door. Haze took the keys and saved her the struggle. Once inside, Gabby's gaze went to the top of the stairs, expecting to hear the same sounds as before. She felt Haze's hand touch her back. Slowly, they went up the stairs. Gabby was glad for Haze being there. *If I had come alone I wouldn't have made it this far.* They stopped at the entrance to the bedroom. Gabby's heart beat painfully in her chest.

"I can't believe I was here just yesterday, watching her cheat on me." She stepped into the room. The bed was unmade, the blinds closed. Nicole's clothes were strewn on the floor. In all likelihood, Nicole hadn't stayed there the night before. "She hasn't even bothered to change the sheets." The framed photo of them lay on its front, as if Nicole hadn't wanted Gabby to watch her cheating. Gabby threw it against the wall, the sound of glass breaking satisfying her rage temporarily. "I'm so fucking angry with her. How am I supposed to forgive her for this?" She motioned around the room. "I don't think I could ever trust her again."

"I don't know what to say." Haze stood just outside the bedroom. "I hate seeing you like this." She stepped inside and glanced around, her eyes narrowing. "If it was anybody else, I'd say run for the hills, but this is Nikki. I've known her thirty years, and she's never done anything like this before. Perhaps she's going through something we don't know about?"

"You're sticking up for her?" Gabby couldn't believe her ears. How could Haze ever try and make this seem normal? "I don't care what she's going through. You don't do that to your wife. Besides, I would know if something was up with her." She shook her head. "No, she's a cheat and a liar, and I never want to see her again."

"Gabby, I wasn't sticking up for her, I just think we should give her a chance to explain herself."

"You can do whatever you like, but I'm not interested in her explanations." Gabby reached into the wardrobe and pulled a duffel bag from the top and began throwing some of her things inside. "She didn't even admit to it, then had the audacity to suggest we were having an affair. So much for being your best friend."

"You're right, I'm sorry." Haze blew out a breath. She approached and squeezed Gabby's shoulder. "I just want you to stop hurting, and I don't know how to help."

Seeing Haze looking so lost threw Gabby for a moment, as if this whole thing was as hard for Haze as it was for her. Maybe it was. She had known Nicole for a very long time. *Haze and I are just as close.* Seeing her two best friends like this must be pulling her in two directions. Taking a breath, she said, "Just let me stay with you and allow me to forget about Nicole for a while. I need some time to sort my head out before I talk to her. You don't need to do any more than that. Just be my friend."

"Okay. No—"

"Let me guess, no problem?"

Haze grinned. "Right."

"Let's hurry up and get out of here. I'm feeling the urge to destroy all her stuff, and I'm not sure I have the energy for it." Between them, they gathered the things Gabby needed and left. For the first time in her life, Gabby didn't know what was to come next. She had always had a plan. Knowing what career she wanted from an early age, she had worked for that goal. She had planned to be married, buy a house, and raise a family. She truly believed everything was going as it should. Nicole having an affair wasn't on her list, and she felt adrift from the future she'd meticulously sought for herself. She was thirty-six, pregnant, and sleeping at a friend's house, a friend she had always felt a little attracted to.

No, definitely not the life she had planned, not anymore.

CHAPTER FOUR

Later that afternoon,

Haze glanced at her phone for the hundredth time. Nikki had texted, asking her to come over. She didn't want to go. She was still so angry over Nikki hurting Gabby the way she had. Haze wasn't sure she would be able to hold her tongue. But she also wanted answers. It was so unlike Nikki to do this sort of thing. Haze wanted to find out what was going on. She looked over at Gabby, who was grading papers on the sofa, her hair tied back in a loose ponytail, using the arm of the couch as a table.

"I, uh, have to pop out and meet a client for an hour or two. Will you be all right while I'm gone?" She hated lying to Gabby but didn't want to upset her about going to see Nikki. Gabby had been distant since they got home, unshed tears clinging to her lashes. Burying herself in work seemed to be the only way she could cope. Haze didn't want to bring it all up again.

Gabby glanced at her and smiled. "Yeah, I'll be fine. I might see what I can pull together from your fridge and cook us a meal for when you get back."

"You don't need to do that." Not only did she not want Gabby to wait on her, but she also knew there really wasn't much in the fridge anyway. A trip to the shop would be in order tomorrow. "Why don't you relax? Take a bath and pamper yourself. Paint your nails or something, or whatever you girls do." She blushed when Gabby smirked at her.

"Haze, you're a woman too."

"Yeah, I know that, but I'm not exactly the feminine type." She looked down at herself. Her customary tank top and faded jeans had seen better days, and the boots by the door could do with new soles. She bit her nails and hardly brushed her short hair. No, no one would ever say she was feminine, and that was fine with her. She liked who she was, but under Gabby's frank perusal, she suddenly felt self-conscious. Would someone like Gabby ever be attracted to her? She thought of Nicole, her long coal-black hair, manicured nails, and expensive suits. Clearly Gabby's type was the opposite of Haze. Haze's only feminine quality was her name, Hazel. She refused to ever be called that.

"And I am?"

"Well, yeah, I mean… You look, well… You know." Haze couldn't get the right words out. Saying Gabby was beautiful wouldn't do her justice. Everything about her was lush. Her full lips, big brown eyes, and curves all lent a sexy quality to her that Haze found ever increasingly irresistible. Add to that her personality, and Haze was a goner.

Gabby laughed loud and long. "For the strong silent type, you sure do blush easily." Haze's blush deepened. "I'm teasing you, Haze." She waved her hand. "Go meet your client, before I embarrass you further."

"I'll see you later." Haze stood quickly and rushed out the door, grateful for the chilly afternoon air to cool the heat in her body. Gabby always got her hot, even without trying. Add flirting into the mix, and Haze didn't think she'd be able to breathe much longer. She knew Gabby wasn't interested in her. The flirting and teasing was just playful, but it still stirred Haze up.

Taking the long way to get to Nikki's, gave her some time to refocus. When Nikki answered the door, Haze couldn't help but gasp. It was clear Nikki hadn't been to bed yet—judging by the dark circles under her eyes. Haze wondered if it was because she was worrying about Gabby or if she had been out screwing all night. She didn't ask.

"I didn't think you'd show up." Nikki opened the door wider for her to enter.

"I wasn't going to, but I really want to know what you were thinking." Haze strode through to the lounge and sat in the armchair, placing her hands under her thighs to stop the tremor that stole through her body. Nikki followed her in and flopped down on the couch.

"Does Gabby know you're here?"

"No. I didn't want to upset her."

Nikki smirked. "She does have quite the temper, doesn't she? I found the smashed picture frame in the bedroom. It took me ages to clear up."

"You're lucky that's the only thing she did." Haze took a breath, noting that Nikki didn't look exactly sorry for what she had done. Does she feel guilty at all? "I can't believe you called her a liar. She isn't stupid; she knows what she saw."

"You're supposed to be my best mate." Nikki narrowed her eyes. "How about you stop sticking up for her and be on my side?"

Was she serious? Did she really think Haze would be on her side in all this? Nikki was the cheat, not Gabby. Best friends or not, Haze had a right to be pissed at her. "I don't want to take sides. I'm friends with you both, but I can't condone what you've done. You've hurt her so much, Nikki. And she's pregnant for Christ's sake."

"Don't you think I know that? I love her."

"You have a funny way of showing it. How could you do this to her?"

Nikki looked away for a second. "Things aren't always what they seem, Haze. Even before the pregnancy, we weren't getting along. We didn't fight, but we'd stopped talking to each other. It felt like all the romance had left."

That was the first Haze heard of problems between them. As far as she knew, things were fine. You didn't plan to get pregnant if there were issues in your marriage, did you? Obviously she didn't expect to be told everything that went on between them, but surely one of them would have said something if there was anything serious going on.

"Isn't that what happens to all marriages after a time? That's no excuse for cheating. If things were that bad, why get pregnant?"

"We both want children. We'd been planning it for a couple of years. Just because we were going through a rough patch shouldn't mean we should give up our dream."

"So what, you thought you could get her pregnant and then screw around on the side?"

"It wasn't like that. Rhea works at the office. She started flirting with me, and it felt nice. I played along. One thing led to another, and it just happened."

Haze stood and went to the window, looking out unseeing. "How long?" She turned and glared at Nikki. "How long have you been messing around?"

Nikki didn't answer for a moment, then blew out a breath. "Seven months."

"For fuck's sake, Nikki! You could have stopped the IVF before it was too late. Now Gabby is pregnant with nowhere to live." How could she do this to her? Allow her to get pregnant when Nikki was already cheating on her. How selfish could you get?

"She can come home."

"You really think she wants to come back here after what she saw? You're crazy."

"We can find somewhere else. I'll tell Rhea it's over. Gabby and I can start again, as a family."

"Good luck trying to convince her of that, she's devastated."

"I fucked up, I know. Please stop giving me a hard time and be my friend."

"Nikki, I love you, you know that. Right now, I don't want to even look at you. I tried to convince Gabby that maybe you were going through something horrible you didn't know how to cope with. It turns out you just wanted a fuck."

Nikki got to her feet and into Haze's personal space, her eyes flashing. "Oh, well I'm sorry, Saint Hazel. Didn't realise you had to climb all the way down off your high horse to speak to me. I bet you're just loving this. You get to comfort Gabby and offer her a place to stay. Won't be long before you're muttering sweet nothings in her ear and getting her pants off."

Haze's hands tightened into fists, but resisted the overwhelming urge to slap her. "That's a new low, even for you."

"Come on, you've been in love with her for as long as I have." Nikki stepped back and sat once again, spreading her arms along the back of the couch like she didn't have a care in the world.

"You're right, I have, but have I ever once crossed that line with her? Done anything to make you think I'd make a move on her? I'd never do that to you. For you to suggest I would shows how much you don't know me at all. You need to sort your shit out if you want her back, but leave me out of it. Gabby is welcome at mine for as long as she likes. I won't fuck her over like you have."

Without waiting for Nikki to respond, Haze stormed out. It was a mistake to come here, to think Nikki might actually say sorry for the mess she's caused. How could the person she had known all her life turn into someone she didn't recognise?

She arrived home soon after, feeling frustrated and confused. She took her boots off and wandered into the house. "Gabby?"

"In the kitchen."

Haze found her sitting at the kitchen table, flipping through takeout menus. Her hair was freshly washed. The scent flared Haze's nostrils. She sat at the opposite side of the table.

"Did you have a nice client meeting?"

"I lied to you. I went to see Nikki."

"I know."

Haze's eyebrows lifted in surprise. "What? How?"

Gabby lifted her mobile from the table's surface and waved it slightly. "She texted me a few minutes ago, asking me not to be angry with you for seeing her."

Haze tried to gauge if Gabby was annoyed with her or not. She couldn't read the vibe. Gabby kept her head down, looking at the menus. Haze needed to see her eyes, but Gabby refused to look up. Haze rested her head in her hand. "She knows I didn't tell you I was going there. She's trying to set me up." *And cause trouble between us.*

"Guess she doesn't know how honourable you are." Gabby finally looked up and smiled. "You told me right away. Why?"

"I figured you've had enough lies told to you recently, I didn't want to add to them."

"Thank you." She glanced away for a moment. "Did she tell you why she cheated? How long it's been going on?"

Haze lifted her head and spread her hands out in front of her. "I'm really in an awkward position here. I could sit here and slag her off, but if you two sort things out and get back together, I'll be the one losing out. I'll be the one who said the horrible things, while you two go off happily together. I don't want to be put in the middle."

"That's fair enough."

Gabby folded her arms across her chest. Haze reached over the table and took her hands in her own. "It's not that I don't want to tell you, I do, I just don't want to be the one to upset you."

"Oh, Haze." Gabby squeezed her fingers. "Whatever she did isn't your fault. I'm bound to be upset, but I'd never take it out on you. Can you answer me one thing though?"

Haze swallowed hard. "If I can."

"How long has it been going on?"

She didn't see the point of lying. No doubt, the truth would come out eventually. "Seven months."

A tear escaped Gabby's eye and rolled down her cheek. "Is it serious?"

"I don't think so."

"Okay. I won't ask anymore. I'll go see her next week sometime and ask her about it then. I won't put you in this position again."

"It's alright."

Gabby shook her head, squeezing her hands again. "No, it's not. You're right, you shouldn't be made a go-between." Gabby let go and picked up a menu. "How about we order a take-away, and you can show me what you're working on?"

"Sounds good."

CHAPTER FIVE

Monday morning, Gabby found Haze sitting at the kitchen table, coffee cup in one hand, a pencil in the other. She was doodling in a sketchbook. Gabby headed for the kettle and set about making tea. She couldn't help her gaze flicking back to her friend repetitively. Haze looked tired, and Gabby wondered how long she had been up. Despite Gabby digging for clues as to what Nikki said, Haze had remained stoic and remote. She'd spent most of the weekend working in her office. Gabby felt swamped with guilt, knowing it was her wife who had put them all in this situation. *Maybe I should take some time off and go stay with my parents.* She grimaced at the thought. As much as she loved her folks, spending any length of time with them was torture. Her mother constantly fussed, and her father was always at the racetrack. Her mother complained about him constantly. *No, I don't want to go there. I want to stay here, with Haze.* Gabby took her tea to the table. Haze looked up and smiled, but didn't greet her. *Maybe she doesn't want me here anymore?*

"What do you have planned for today?" Gabby asked.

"I have a few errands to run, then a meeting with the dog walkers to show them my designs." Haze glanced up and went back drawing in her book. "Are you nervous about going in to work?"

"A little." Gabby shrugged, then sighed. "You know Edith; she hates when staff don't follow her orders. I texted her yesterday to say I was okay and apologised for missing the meeting. She wants to see me first thing."

"What will you tell her?"

"As close to the truth as possible, family emergency and hope she doesn't ask for details."

"You know you don't have to tell her anything, right?" Haze put down her pencil, giving her full attention to Gabby, with a gaze full of concern.

"Yeah, I know, but she's been good to me since she took over as headteacher. I respect her. I don't want her feeling like I've let her down."

"That's crazy."

Gabby shrugged. "Can't help the way I feel."

Haze reached across the table and squeezed her hand where it rested on the surface. "You'll be fine. Give me a text or call later, if you like, let me know how it goes."

"Okay." Gabby smiled, seeing the genuine support in her expression. Haze had always been like that. Always supporting her with whatever she was dealing with. She was the kindest person Gabby knew, and the only person she'd gone to with her concerns about getting pregnant. She hadn't even shared her reservations with Nicole. After one hour of talking it through with Haze, Gabby's decision was made. She had no regrets. Having children had always been in her life plan. A few wobbles wouldn't stop her from achieving her goals. *But what now? My wife is a cheater.*

"Have you heard from Nikki at all?"

Gabby drew her brows down against the image of Nikki with her lover. Seven months! Would she ever be able to forget the visual? She hoped so. If they had any chance of reconciling, that moment when Gabby caught her cheating would need to vanish. No way could she live with Nicole, if all she could see was her screwing someone else.

"She's tried calling, but I let it go to voicemail. As much as I hate her right now, I think I should go see her later, see if she can help me understand why she did it."

"That's a good idea." Haze picked up her pencil again and finished her sketch. "I'll be here when you get home."

Gabby watched for a moment. Haze pulled her lower lip between her teeth, as she concentrated on her task. Occasionally, Haze's gaze would find Gabby and then return to the paper.

"I'm sorry for all this."

Haze frowned. "Hey, not your fault. Hopefully, you two can sort things out and get back on track."

"Do you really think I should do that? How could I trust her again?"

"I honestly don't know, but you guys are married and expecting a kid." She put the pencil down again and smiled. "Isn't it worth a try to see if you can work things out?"

Gabby glanced at the sketchbook. Her own image smiled up from the paper. *She's been sketching me.* Even with

Gabby's limited knowledge in art, it wasn't hard to see how well Haze had drawn her. She had made Gabby look beautiful. "Is that what you want? For us to get back together?"

Haze looked away for a second, her cheeks tinting pink. She seemed almost embarrassed by the question. She cleared her throat. "It's nothing to do with me. I'm just here as your friend."

"You're more than that," Gabby whispered, her eyes going wide when she realised what she had said.

"Gabby..."

"Sorry. I best get going. See you later."

Gabby stood too quickly in her effort to escape Haze's pleading look. Her head spun. She had no idea why she had said that. It wasn't like she wanted anything to happen between them. Gabby loved her wife, but sharing space with Haze had stirred up that old attraction. There was just something about Haze that fascinated Gabby. Every time she looked at her, her stomach would give a low roll. It had always been that way. Over the years, she had learned to control it, telling herself it was admiration for Haze's strength and beauty. She thought of Nicole, of the years they had shared together. Did she ever inspire that reaction? In the beginning, but it had faded over time. Gabby supposed that was what happened in all long-term partnerships. They were a loving couple, had planned a future together, and were now having a baby. Despite what Nicole had done, they had time and effort in their life together. It would be stupid to throw it all away just because Gabby couldn't control her hormones. It wasn't fair to Haze, and it wasn't fair to Nicole. Gabby would never cheat on her. Until they sorted their problems out, Gabby would need to keep her errant libido in check.

†

Forty minutes later, Gabby knocked on Edith's office door, her body trembling with anxiety. She didn't want to get into the state of her home life, but she also didn't want to lie to her friend and boss.

"Come in," Edith called from inside. "Ah, Gabriella. Take a seat. It's good to see you're alive. We were worried about you."

Gabby sat in the guest chair, resting her hands over her bump, and smiled at Edith. Edith was well into her sixties. She wore her hair in a severe bun and her clothes looked old fashioned, but her face still held a youthful appearance that Gabby was immensely jealous of.

"I'm sorry. I received a phone call from a family member with an emergency, and I had to leave."

"Without telling your wife?" Edith quirked an eyebrow. "When I spoke to her she didn't have a clue where you were."

"Oh, yeah, I um, didn't have time to call her in my rush to leave. I spoke to her later that night." Gabby shifted in her seat, as Edith gazed at her through narrowed lids. It was obvious she didn't believe her. Gabby had never been any good at lying, and Edith was shrewd enough to spot one a mile away.

"Gabby, I like to think we're friends." She folded her hands on the desk and leaned forward, smiling softly. "If there is anything you need or want to talk about, I'm here for you."

"Thank you, Edie. I promise, if there comes a time I need to, I will."

"Good enough. Let me get you the minutes from the meeting and discuss the role I would like you to play in organising the end-of-year play."

Gabby was pleased Edith didn't press further. She needed time to talk to Nicole, to figure out where they were going, before she told anyone about it all. As much as she trusted Edith, there was no point telling her the gory details if she and Nicole worked things out. Gabby didn't want to embarrass Nicole if there was no need to. Nicole would often accompany Gabby to school functions, and it would do no good to have people at the school know her business. Not that she owed Nicole anything, not after what she had done, but it wasn't in Gabby's nature to be spiteful just for the sake of it.

CHAPTER SIX

Five thirty that evening, Gabby pulled up to her home. Her stomach clenched the same as it had Saturday morning when she had collected her things. The trepidation of what she might find on the other side of the door unnerved her, not that she thought she would catch Nicole cheating again. Even Nicole wasn't that stupid, especially knowing Gabby was on her way over to talk. Still, the feelings lingered. As she walked up the pathway, the front door opened. Nicole smiled brightly as if she hadn't done anything wrong. Gabby pressed her lips tight together, to stop herself from commenting. She was determined to get an explanation from Nicole before her anger exploded. It was the hardest thing she had ever done.

"Gabby, thanks for coming." Nicole stepped aside so Gabby could pass.

"I didn't do it for you. I need to understand a few things." Gabby walked into the lounge. She avoided looking at the stairs, and sat in the leather armchair Haze had bought them when they moved in. She felt connected to Haze sitting there, and it offered her comfort. Nicole slouched on the sofa, pulling her legs up and resting her head in her hand.

"Of course. Do you want a drink or anything?"

"No, I want to know how many times you've cheated on me in the last seven months." Nicole didn't even flinch at the question. Gabby knew, in that instant, her marriage was probably over.

"Haze told you, then?"

"Only the minimum, and I had to pry that out of her. It's not fair to stick her in the middle of all this."

"Already defending her, I see." Nicole's eyes narrowed, as she pursed her lips.

"She's our friend. Of course I'm going to defend her, but this isn't about Haze." She waved her hand dismissively. "How many times?"

"Christ, Gabby, I don't know." Nicole looked away, frowning.

"Two times? Ten, twenty? Come on, you must have some idea." As much as it hurt to ask these questions, Gabby had to know everything.

Nicole shrugged. "More than twenty, I guess."

Gabby closed her eyes, bile rising in her throat. How had she not known what Nicole was up to? Her hand involuntarily went to her bump, as if she was shielding the baby from the truth of Nicole's duplicity. "When you were staying late at work?"

Nicole nodded.

"The weekend I went home to see my parents, and you had an emergency client meeting and couldn't come with me?"

She nodded again.

"I can't believe this. I thought we were in love, happy."

Nicole stood and went to the lounge window, staring out into the fading light, her back to Gabby. "We are, but you have to admit things have been a little strained recently."

"No, I don't." This was news to Gabby. She thought things between them were the same as always. They both worked hard and spent the evenings catching up on their days, talking about future plans, and cooking meals together. Nothing seemed out of the ordinary to Gabby. "As far as I knew, we were perfectly happy, planning the baby."

"But we didn't make love anymore, didn't cuddle up on the sofa." Nicole spun around accusation in her eyes. "You seemed distant, and I didn't know how to fix it."

"Nothing was wrong, it's called life. Not everything is about sex. Though apparently for you it is. What happened, Nic? We had our future planned. How could you let me get pregnant if you were unhappy?"

"We wanted kids."

"But you were fucking someone else," she bellowed. What on earth possessed Nicole to think that sleeping with someone else whilst planning for a baby was any way to have a happy marriage? Nicole shrugged again and lifted her arms, as if to say so what.

"I don't know what you want me to say."

"Sorry would be a good start."

"I'm sorry."

Restless energy filled Gabby. She rose from the chair and paced the small room. "Are you though? Because you don't look like it." She stopped and glared at Nicole. "Where were you Friday night? I know you didn't sleep here." Nicole looked away and didn't answer.

"You were with her, weren't you?"

"Yes."

"I don't believe this."

Nicole's eyes narrowed again, she pointed angrily at Gabby. "You can talk, getting all cosy with Haze."

What? "Oh my God." She threw her hands in the air. "Why do you keep insisting there is something going on with Hazel and me?"

"Because I think there is. She's always loved you."

"But I love you, well, I did."

"She was the first person you went to."

"Because she's my friend."

"No, there's more to it. I've seen the way you look at her. You forget, I know how you look when you're attracted to someone."

"So this is my fault?" Nicole had always been good at reading people, but Gabby thought she had hidden her attraction to Haze well over the years. Just because you were attracted to someone didn't mean you wanted to be with them. Gabby had chosen Nicole. To accuse her now of being in love with someone else wasn't fair. "Yes, Haze is good looking, but I married you. I have always been faithful to you." She touched her growing bump. "I'm having your baby for Christ's sake."

"I can't help but think you two are better suited. I've always thought that."

"But I'm with you." *How many times do I have to repeat myself?*

"That doesn't mean you don't wish you were with her."

"Have I done or said something to make you think that?" Gabby sat back in the chair, closing her eyes for a moment.

"Not really, just a feeling I have."

"So you decided to cheat on me first, is that it?"

Nicole shrugged.

"Haze is just a friend. You should have talked to me about this before you decided to go fuck someone else. Before I got pregnant."

"I didn't know how."

"That's a lame excuse, and I'm not buying this jealousy act. You're trying to turn it around on me, so I feel guilty and forgive you. It's not happening. You cheated on me, not the other way around."

"Are you saying you're not attracted to her?"

"I'm your wife." *Why does she keep on trying to blame me for all this? I didn't do anything wrong.*

"That's not an answer."

Gabby couldn't answer her. To do that would give Nicole the ammunition to turn it around on Gabby. Gabby had always been committed to Nicole, despite her awareness of Haze.

"You are, aren't you?" Nicole moved closer, placing her hands on the arms of the chair, leaning over Gabby. "I knew it. Have you slept with her yet?"

Gabby's arm shot out and slapped her hard across the cheek, causing Nicole to stumble back. "How dare you?" She stood from the chair. "I don't want to see you for a while. We need to take a break, figure out if we have a future together. Right now, I can't see one. You made this mess, and only you can figure it out. If you sleep with her again, we're over for good." She slammed through the door and got into her car, her body vibrating with anger. Of all the things to accuse her of, sleeping with Haze would have been the last one Gabby would have thought of.

As she drove, doubt crept into her mind. Had it really been that obvious Gabby was attracted to Haze? Did she somehow cause Nicole to have misgivings about their own relationship, only finding comfort in another woman's arms? She thought back over the years. Gabby couldn't find one time she had ever acted inappropriately with Haze. Every night out, weekends away, or movie nights, Gabby had always been cuddled up to Nicole. When they made love, she never once pictured Haze. It was always Nicole who surrounded her, bringing her to orgasm. Yes, Haze had kissed her once, and yes, it was amazing. Gabby had spent ten years loving Nicole. No, this was just Nicole's way of laying the blame at her feet. Nicole was the liar and the cheat, not Gabby.

She got back to Haze's thirty minutes later, finding her stretched out on the couch watching TV. Gabby kicked off her shoes and hung up her coat, then sat next to Haze.

"How'd it go?" Haze muted the television.

"Not great." Gabby let her head fall back, closing her eyes and letting out a sigh. "She gave me the same story as you, about me being distant and whatnot. A load of bullshit." Gabby felt Haze's eyes on her. She tilted her head to meet her gaze. Gabby thought Haze could see right into her soul.

"There's something else. What is it?" Haze asked softly.

"It doesn't matter." Gabby shook her head. How could she tell Haze that Nicole thought they were sleeping together?

"It does matter, because you're upset." Haze reached out, laying her hand on Gabby's thigh. "What did she say?"

A tremor stole through Gabby's body the moment Haze touched her, causing Gabby to flinch. That was the first time in years Haze's touch had generated that reaction. Gabby put it down to her hormones and Nicole's insistence something was going on between them. It definitely wasn't because Gabby's attraction to Haze had intensified in the last few days.

"What happened to not wanting to be in the middle of all this?" She stood and headed to the kitchen, as far away from Haze as she could get. Haze followed. "It's none of your business, Haze," Gabby pleaded.

"Okay. Just trying to help." Haze's eyes dimmed and she looked away, lowering her head.

"Shit, I'm sorry."

"It's fine, you're right. It has nothing to do with me." Haze turned to go.

"Not according to Nicole." Gabby spoke softly.

"Excuse me?"

"Damn." Gabby hadn't realised she had said that out loud. "Okay, you have to promise not to get mad."

"What about me?"

Gabby warred with herself for a minute. This is such a bad idea. "Nicole reckons that the reason I was off with her and not wanting to be intimate with her was that I was attracted to you. She thinks I want to be with you."

Haze's eyes went wide, her mouth falling open in clear shock. "That's crazy."

"Is it? All the way home I couldn't help but think maybe, on some level, she was right."

"Gabby, no. You've always loved Nikki. You're having her baby."

"All true, but you have to know there has always been a spark between us." What am I doing? I just spent the last hour denying I had feelings for Haze and now I'm begging her to admit we have a connection? Idiot!

"Just because you're physically attracted to someone doesn't mean you want to act on it. We're friends. That's all. You love Nikki."

"You're right, I do. I told her we were just friends, but I don't think she believed me."

"Well, she'll have to, because that's all we are and all we'll ever be. Do you still love her?"

"Yeah, even though I know what she's done, I can't just shut my feelings off." She did still love Nicole, but did that mean she wanted to be with her again? After their little showdown, Gabby didn't think so.

"Then work it out. You have the chance to have a proper family, don't ruin that because she put some stupid idea in your head. We're friends."

"The best of friends."

"Yeah, and that's all we'll be."

"Yes, just friends." Holding her friend's gaze, Gabby couldn't help but think they were heading toward something, something she didn't want to fight anymore. Haze was strong, capable, and determined, as well as sexy. They all knew Haze loved Gabby. Did Gabby love Haze in the same way? Was it worth fighting for her marriage with a cheater when Haze was looking at her with such devotion?

The baby kicked, bringing Gabby back to reality. Haze was a fantasy, a game of what if. Gabby had made a commitment to Nicole, and she wouldn't throw that away with some long-lost hope of being with Haze. They had all made their choices. It was time to act like the grownups they were. Whether Gabby got back together with Nicole or not, she had a baby on the way. That was the most important concern. She would need to figure things out soon before the baby arrived. Gabby didn't want to be sleeping in someone else's home with a newborn. Her child would need stability, a home. Perhaps it was time to ask Nicole to move out and allow Gabby her home back. Why should Gabby be the one homeless, when Nicole was the cheater?

CHAPTER SEVEN

Haze stood at the cooker, hands on the worktop. She was staring at the pot of potatoes and waiting for the water to boil. Gabby had gone for a nap shortly after their chat. Haze couldn't blame her; she looked worn out. Dark shadows ringed her eyes, and her normally tan skin had lost its pallor. Haze still couldn't get her head around the fact Nikki had cheated on Gabby. Their relationship had seemed solid. That wasn't the only thing on Haze's mind. Having Gabby confess to a spark between them had thrown her. Haze felt it too, always had, but that admission was just biology on Gabby's part. Gabby had always been in love with Nicole. Or had she?

Haze turned down the heat when bubbles filled the pan, then checked the chicken in the oven. With everything cooking as it should, she sat at the table and flipped open her sketchbook. Gabby's image stared back at her. She gently traced Gabby's jawline, careful not to smudge the pencil marks. How was it fair that someone as beautiful as Gabby ended up with someone like Nikki? A cheater. *If I hadn't have been such a coward all those years ago, hadn't run off, would Gabby be with me now?* It was a question she couldn't answer. When Gabby had talked over her meeting with Nikki, about Nikki accusing them of sleeping together, Haze couldn't miss the hint of longing in Gabby's gaze. Was Gabby really hiding feelings for her?

It didn't matter. Haze wasn't going to get in their way. Gabby and Nikki needed to sort themselves out—especially with a baby on the way. Haze wouldn't be the one to break up that family. She herself was a child of divorce, and she hated always being in the middle of her parents' arguments. No, she wouldn't do that to Gabby's baby.

The timer on the cooker dinged. Haze set about plating up the roast chicken and vegetables. "Gabby? Dinner is ready," she called, knowing Gabby would hear her in the small apartment. She removed her sketchbook and set the plates on either side of the table.

"Ah great, I'm starving." Gabby's nap she hadn't diminished the exhaustion in her features. "This all looks wonderful. It must have taken you ages to prepare."

"Not really." Haze shrugged and picked up her knife and fork.

"You cooked my favourite."

"I figured you could do with some comfort food." Haze felt the heat rise to her cheeks.

"Thank you. You're amazing."

"Just being a good hostess." Haze's blush deepened. There was nothing Gabby liked more than roast chicken and steamed veg, the most basic of recipes. It always warmed Haze how simple and low maintenance Gabby was. She was never one to go out clubbing, always preferring to stay in and watch movies. Haze couldn't count how many evenings she'd spent at Gabby and Nikki's house watching DVD's and chopping veg together. Nikki always tried to get them to go out, but Haze was content to stay in with Gabby. Perhaps that's why Nikki thinks we're better suited as a couple? I always did like hanging around Gabby more than Nikki. Despite Nikki being her friend for thirty years, Haze had more in common with Gabby. Not wanting to think too much about their history, she asked, "How did you get on at work?"

"It was fine. I told Edith I had a family thing. I don't think she bought it, but she didn't question me further."

"That's good."

Gabby smiled. "Yeah, although I don't like lying to her." She sipped her water. "She's a good friend, not just my boss, but the thought of telling her I couldn't keep my wife from straying doesn't fill me with glee." Gabby's eyes began to glisten. She rose from the table and fetched a napkin, holding it against her eyelids. Haze put her cutlery down, her appetite vanishing. It tore her heart to see Gabby so upset.

"Hey, this isn't your fault. You did nothing wrong."

"I can't help thinking that maybe I did." Gabby threw the napkin onto the countertop. Her forehead creased deeply with her frown. "I should have paid her more attention, gave in when she wanted to make love." She shrugged. "Maybe she's right. Maybe I'm not as attracted to her as I once was, and getting pregnant was just an excuse to occupy our time."

"Do you really believe that?"

"I don't know what to believe." Gabby's arms lifted then dropped to her sides. "I just can't get my head around it all. When I saw her earlier, she didn't even look sorry. She seemed almost proud of it. That isn't the Nicole I know. She looked like a stranger." She leaned back against the sink, defeat in her features. "Haze, I really think my marriage is over. I always imagined, if someone got caught cheating, they would beg and plead to be forgiven. I had to prompt her to say sorry." She looked away, drawing in a big breath and releasing it on a sigh. "I don't think she loves me anymore."

Seeing the tears run down Gabby's cheeks was all the motivation Haze needed to stand and approach her. "Come here." She gathered Gabby close, cupping the back of her head as Gabby leaned into her chest.

"Why is this happening now?" Gabby's voice was muffled. Her warm breath on Haze's neck triggered Haze's stomach to clench. "I can't be a single parent. I'm not strong enough."

"Hey." Haze tilted Gabby's head so she could catch her gaze. "You're the strongest person I know. And you won't be alone. If it doesn't work out with Nikki, you'll always have me. I won't leave you."

"You promise?"

"Yes," Haze whispered. Their faces were inches apart. It would be so easy for Haze to give in to her desires and kiss her. She stepped back, ignoring the confusion in Gabby's gaze as she moved away.

"You're Nicole's best friend. I can't come between you."

Haze shook her head. "I'm not sure we are friends anymore. After what she said to me…"

"What?"

54

"It doesn't matter."

Gabby reached out and gently touched Haze's forearm, bringing goosebumps to her skin. "It does if she's upset you."

"It's okay, really." Haze moved farther away, then sat back at the table. "I don't want to see her for a while, not until she apologises." Nikki accusing her of trying to get with Gabby hurt more than she dared to admit. *Yeah, I've been in love with Gabby for as long as I can remember, but I'd never come between them. Nikki knows that.* As heart-wrenching as it was for Haze to put aside her feelings for Gabby, it was the right thing to do. She wouldn't be the one to break up a family.

Their food had grown cold. They attempted to eat but mainly pushed it around on their plates.

"I don't think we'll ever know why she did this." Gabby suddenly broke the silence. "She's changed. She's not the woman I married, and I'm not sure I like this new version."

"Me neither."

Gabby sighed and pushed her plate away. Haze did the same. "Thank you for dinner. Is it okay if I take a bath?"

"Of course. Treat this like your home."

"Thanks. Leave the dishes, I'll do them later."

"Okay."

Haze watched her leave, then slumped back in the chair, running a hand through her hair. Maybe Gabby living here isn't the best idea. It was easy to keep her feelings in check when the object of her affection lived miles away. Gabby had only been there three days. Already, Haze's libido was screaming at her to make a move. There were only so many times Haze could stare into those wounded eyes, before she would do something stupid to take Gabby's pain away.

Maybe Nikki was right in thinking about my motivations for allowing Gabby to stay. Maybe I'm just as bad as the cheater.

†

Haze ignored Gabby's request and did the dishes. While her mind churned, she realised she had distanced herself from Gabby and Nikki over the last few months. They would usually spend at least one night a week together, but since the pregnancy Haze couldn't be around them. Seeing the woman she loved carrying someone else's baby was torture. If only Haze had found out about Nikki cheating sooner. Maybe she could have stopped the implantation and avoided this whole mess. Then again, having children was always in Gabby's future. The situation might not be ideal, but the baby was coming. Haze couldn't wait to meet the little one. Gabby would be a great mother. Haze just hoped that Nikki would sort herself out by the time the baby arrived, so she could be a mother too. Nikki had a lot of making up to do, especially to Gabby. From the look in Gabby's eyes earlier, Haze didn't think she would ever forgive Nikki for cheating. What a mess.

She put away the last of the dishes, then headed to her bedroom to grab a load of dirty laundry. All the thinking in the world wouldn't resolve the issues they were all facing. Until Nikki made amends, they would be stuck in limbo.

Haze pushed open the door and sucked in a breath. Her skin heated instantly at the sight before her. Gabby stood by her open duffel bag, lifting out a nightshirt, completely naked. Her skin was smooth and glistened in the lamplight, still damp from her bath. Gabby spun around at Haze's interruption. Wide eyed, she lifted the shirt to cover her round, heavy breasts. Her swollen belly only added to her sexiness. Haze couldn't breathe. Never before had she been so turned on by a woman. Gabby was breathtaking.

"Haze!"

Haze blinked. She lifted her gaze from the triangle of hair at the juncture of Gabby's thighs to her face. "Shit. Sorry. I thought you were still in the bathroom."

Gabby tilted her head to the side and smiled, appearing amused at Haze's discomfort. "It's okay. You might want to turn around though."

"Shit. Sorry." Haze turned around and fled, mortified she had been staring at Gabby like a horny teenager. How could she not? Gabby was gorgeous. Her pregnancy had lent a softness to her body. She radiated beauty. Haze paced the small kitchen, her hands gripping her head. *This isn't going to work. I can't live here seeing her all the time. I nearly came just from looking at her.*

"Haze? Are you okay?" Haze hadn't noticed Gabby standing at the threshold to the kitchen, leaning against the archway. Thankfully, she was now covered in a long T-shirt, which stopped mid-thigh. "You're trembling."

"I'm fine." She tried to smile confidently but knew it came out in a grimace. "I'm great."

Gabby frowned and took a step closer. Haze backed up.

"Haze, what's going on?"

"Nothing. Just wasn't expecting to see you, um…You know." She waved vaguely at Gabby.

"Naked?"

"Yeah."

Gabby grinned. "You've seen me naked before."

"But that was after the gym and stuff." Plenty of times they had changed in front of each other, but Haze always refrained from staring too much. She would dress and leave as quickly as she could. Walking in now to see Gabby in all her glory was unexpected, and that was why she was transfixed.

"How is this any different?"

Because I saw everything! "It's not. You're right." She brushed past Gabby. "I'm going to head into my office for a bit before I go to bed." She had to escape. She needed to get her hormones under control. "Goodnight, Gabby."

Gabby reached out and grabbed her arm, preventing her from leaving. "Haze. Was it different because Nicole and I are separated and your feelings for me are coming out stronger?"

Haze snatched her arm back. "Why would you ask me that? You know I don't see you that way."

"But you do. Haze, we all know it."

Gabby stepped closer, her fresh scent jumbling Haze's thoughts. "Why are you doing this to me?"

"Doing what?" Gabby's tone had dropped to a near whisper. The husky quality made Haze's insides squirm.

"Confusing me."

Gabby stepped closer still. Only a few inches separated them. "Is that what I'm doing?"

"Yes. You know how I feel, yet you keep tormenting me even though there's no chance of anything happening."

"What makes you think there's no chance?" Gabby entwined their fingers.

Haze stared down into Gabby's brown eyes, their liquid depths pulling her in. "Three days ago you were happily in love with Nikki."

"You're right, I was. All that's changed now. We're not together, and I can't see that altering." Gabby reached up and cupped Haze's cheek. "Why can't we do what I know you're dying to do?"

"Because we aren't those people." Haze moved away, losing the warmth of Gabby immediately. "You need to sort out your relationship with Nikki and leave me alone. I won't be used for a distraction because you're feeling down about yourself."

"Is that what you think? That I'm using you?"

Yes. "Do you love Nikki?"

Gabby looked away, her brows pinched. "I don't know anymore." When she looked back, her eyes were almost desperate.

It would be so easy to give in to her need, to take Gabby right there and then. She couldn't, wouldn't, be used that way.

"But, Haze, you and I could be great together."

"I've been in love with you for as long as I can remember." This was the first time she had acknowledged those feelings aloud to Gabby. Yes, they all knew she loved her, but Haze had never said it to Gabby before. "A one-night stand would never be enough for me. And screw you for thinking it would." Haze walked away.

"Haze."

Haze spun around, her body vibrating with anger. *How dare she think I'd sleep with her this way.* "No. You chose Nikki. I'm not going to be your sloppy seconds just because she cheated on you. Besides, I have a date Friday night with someone I really like." A lie, but it was the only way to stop this. Let Gabby think she had interest elsewhere. "She could be the one, you know."

"Oh, okay." Gabby's gaze dropped to the carpet, her shoulders slumping. "I hope you have a nice time." She glanced up then away, her skin flushing. "Do you want me to leave? If this is too hard for you, I'll talk to Nicole about her moving out and me going back home."

"Is that what you want?"

"No." She shook her head. "The thought of going back in there makes me feel sick, but if my being here is causing you to be upset, I'll go."

Haze should probably tell her to leave. Having her here is driving me crazy, and it's only been three days. Gabby stood there, looking shamefaced and vulnerable. The hurt pulled at Haze's heart. As much as this was killing her, she couldn't let her friend go somewhere that would crush her. "I told you, you can stay here as long as you like. Just, please, forget about there ever being anything between us. We're friends."

Gabby smiled sadly, only a dim light in her eyes. "Okay. Goodnight."

She quickly walked past in the direction of the bedroom, leaving Haze adrift in the living room. Why is all this happening now? Haze wasn't so sure that Gabby would be using her. The wounded look in her eyes when Haze said no was as if being with Haze was something Gabby really wanted. Maybe this thing with Nikki was the catalyst for Haze and Gabby to acknowledge their attraction and to be together properly. Not that it mattered. It had only been three days. For all Haze knew, Gabby would still go back to Nikki. No way could she sleep with her just to have Gabby return to building a family with her wife. That would kill Haze. *I guess I need to find a date for Friday night.* Hopefully Gabby seeing Haze with someone else would end the ridiculousness of Gabby coming on to her again.

CHAPTER EIGHT

Gabby closed the bedroom door with a soft click, then sat on the edge of the bed. Stupid, stupid, stupid. *What the hell was I thinking?* Was Haze right? Was Gabby using her because Nicole had cheated and made her feel worthless? Gabby thought back to the lust that flowed from Haze as she stared at her nakedness. Gabby's skin had flushed, her nipples tightening under the shirt she held up to cover them. There was no mistaking the need in Haze, and it had turned Gabby on something wicked. Nicole had never looked at her with such passion. Gabby hadn't intended to seduce Haze, but seeing her all worked up in the kitchen had lit a flame within. All she wanted was to have Haze's hands on her skin, feel those lips on her mouth. She could see Haze was close to breaking, to giving in to her need, but she had said no.

61

Bringing up Nicole had doused the flame in Gabby with a bucket of cold reality. Yes, she loved her wife, but she didn't want to go back to her, not after everything that had happened. Why couldn't Haze see Gabby was serious and not just using her?

She laid back on the bed, listening to Haze bang around her office down the hall. Gabby hadn't been fair. Using Haze's feelings for her to get her into bed was cruel. Gabby's heart thrummed wildly, as she remembered the look of devastation in Haze's eyes. She would need to apologise and try and explain how she felt. Three days ago, Gabby had been in love with Nicole. That fled the moment she caught Nicole in bed with another woman. Perhaps the shock had blown the cover off her attraction for Haze, allowed it to surface. Nicole was right, Gabby had always been attracted to Haze. She had hidden those feelings well. Now she was no longer with Nicole, what was wrong with exploring things with Haze? Was it really too soon for that? Do I really want to get into a relationship with Haze, when I still don't know what's happening with Nicole? Not that it mattered. Haze apparently had a date Friday night.

A loud bang, followed by Haze cursing, echoed through the wall. Gabby knocked on the closed office door.

"Haze? Everything okay?"

"Yeah. I just dropped something."

Gabby pursed her lips and pressed her head against the wood panelling. "Can we talk for a minute?" Haze probably wanted to be alone after the debacle twenty minutes ago, but Gabby needed to apologise. She didn't want them to go to bed with this between them.

"I'm not really in the mood."

"Please, Haze." Gabby heard movement behind the door, which was then pulled open. It was clear Haze had been crying. The whites of her eyes were red. Tears still clung to her long lashes. "I'm sorry."

"For what?"

"My head is all over the place right now. I shouldn't have come on to you. But I won't deny that I'm attracted to you. I always have been."

"But?"

"But, you're right. Now isn't the time. I have to sort things out with Nicole and think about the baby. If anything was to happen between us, it would have to be after that."

"I told you, I'm not interested."

Gabby's gaze roamed over Haze. She stood ramrod straight, her hands curled into tight fists. Palpable tension buzzed all around her. Haze had always been strong and carefree. Gabby had never seen her so out of sorts before. *It's all my fault.* As much as Gabby wanted to explore things with Haze, it wasn't fair to do this to her. She reached out and ran the back of her fingers down Haze's cheek and watched her eyes close at the contact.

"I won't put you in that position again. I apologise. Let's just forget it ever happened and go back to being friends."

The warm breath Haze released gently coated Gabby's face.

"Thank you." Haze grinned. "I'll go into town tomorrow and get a lock for the bedroom door. We don't want a repeat of earlier, do we?"

I do. "Good idea." Gabby turned away and headed back to her room, her brain more confused than ever. As she settled under the covers it wasn't thoughts of Nicole's betrayal that kept her awake. It was Haze's hooded eyes and sexy grin that tormented her.

†

Haze and Gabby settled into a comfortable routine over the next few days. Gabby would come home from work, they'd chat about their days, and they would cook together. They never spoke of Nicole, which was fine with Gabby. It had been a full week since Gabby had come home and found her cheating. The disbelief was still there, but the anger had begun to dissipate. She was now filled with an overwhelming sadness that her marriage was over. Nicole hadn't even been in contact since their meeting Monday evening. Gabby found she didn't really care. All her thoughts were wrapped up in Haze. Spending the evenings together felt natural, despite tensions being high due to their shared attraction. They refrained from their normal banter. Gabby supposed it was safer that way. She still caught Haze gazing at her longingly, but Haze would turn away, hiding her feelings once again. Despite what Haze said, Gabby couldn't help but think they were heading toward something. Every innocent touch, every glance and smile, filled Gabby with a sense of belonging she hadn't felt since the early days of dating Nicole.

The relatively good mood she'd held all week soured Friday evening. She came home and remembered Haze had a date. Jealousy swamped her. She had seen Haze out with other women before. Why should it irk her now? Probably because I find myself falling for her.

Gabby slammed the front door. This thing with Haze was driving her crazy and spiraling her bad mood. That wasn't her only trouble. She hadn't felt the baby kick since the previous day, and now she was worried. She dumped her coat on the sofa and strode up the hallway.

"Gabby?" Haze poked her head out of the office door, looking all kinds of sexy in her tight black jeans and crisp white shirt. She was obviously ready for her date. "Hey. How was work?"

"Tiring." Gabby couldn't help her gaze lighting over Haze's body. "It seems like every student wanted to act up today. I'm going to head to the bedroom and do some marking." She carried on walking.

"I was thinking about steaks for dinner before I go out. Sound good?"

Gabby didn't look back. "You sort yourself out. I'll just grab a sandwich later." She wasn't really in the mood for food. Her concerns over the baby left her nauseous.

"Are you okay?"

Gabby hadn't heard Haze move and was surprised to find her close with a hand on her lower back. The feel of those fingers created a tremor in her body. She glanced over her shoulder. "I'm fine. Just a long day. Thanks."

"No problem."

Haze dropped her hand, and Gabby escaped into her room. She threw her bag down and kicked off her shoes, settling on the bed. Her hands went to her belly, pressing down in different places, trying to illicit movement from the baby. Nothing. Her arms dropped to the mattress. She wasn't sure how long she'd laid there when a sharp pain gripped her stomach. It eased off then came again. Cramping. Oh God, I'm losing the baby!

Tears fell from her eyes, as she pulled on her trainers. She rushed to get Haze, finding her staring into the fridge.

"Haze?"

Haze turned her head. She slammed the fridge door and rushed to Gabby's side, just as she doubled over clutching her belly. "Gabby? What is it?"

Gabby breathed deeply, trying to ease the pain in her stomach. She glanced up. "Can you take me to the hospital? I haven't felt the baby kick all day, and now I'm cramping." Sobs broke free. She grabbed Haze's hand. "I think I'm losing the baby."

"Oh, God." Haze pulled her to the front door. She helped Gabby put on her coat, then led her to the car. "Everything will be fine," she said, as she sped away from the curb.

The drive to the hospital was a blur for Gabby. Haze pulled up outside the maternity unit in the only spare space and ushered Gabby along into the building. Gabby gripped Haze's hand, the other rubbing her bump. The cramping had eased a little but was still present. Her mind blanked.

"This is Gabriella Turner. We phoned ahead about her pregnancy."

A young man clacked his keyboard, then handed Haze a visitor's pass. He buzzed the lock on the door, and said, "Follow me." Gabby allowed Haze to lead the way. The clerk showed them to a waiting room which, thankfully, was empty. Hopefully, it wouldn't take long to be seen. "Take a seat, and someone will be with you shortly."

The wall in front of Gabby could have been outer space. She stared straight ahead, only vaguely aware of Haze to her right, holding her hand. Dried tears painted her cheeks with resignation to her baby's death. Was this her punishment for allowing feelings for Haze to surface? *Perhaps it's because if I had known about Nicole's cheating earlier, I wouldn't have gone through with the implantation.* None of it mattered. Her baby was dead.

"How are you feeling?" Haze squeezed Gabby's fingers.

Gabby blinked and turned her head. Haze's eyes were clouded with worry, her brows pinched. "I'm still cramping, but it's not as bad as before."

"Has the baby moved at all?"

Gabby shook her head. *Did I wait too long? I should have come first thing this morning. If I did, could I have stopped this from happening?*

"I think I should call Nikki."

"No!" Gabby gripped Haze's hand tighter. "Please, just stay with me." She didn't want Nicole with her. She wanted Haze. Haze with her calm demeanour and quiet strength. Nicole would only worry. She never was any good in a crisis, unless it was in the boardroom.

"Are you sure?" Haze didn't look convinced.

Gabby nodded. "I'm sorry if I ruined your date."

Haze's brows lifted. "What? Don't be stupid. You're far more important than a date."

A mid-forties woman approached, carrying a clipboard. "Ms. Turner? I'm Sally. One of the nurses here. Follow me please." Gabby followed the woman to another room, where ten or twelve cubicles were sectioned off. Privacy curtains shielded three occupants and their own personal tragedies. "Hop up onto the bed." Gabby took off her coat. She handed it to Haze, then settled onto the mattress. Haze sat in an adjacent chair. "When was the last time you felt the baby move?" The nurse lifted Gabby's shirt, then rolled a monitor over to the bedside.

"Right before bed, last night."

"And is baby usually active?" Sally probed Gabby's belly.

"Doesn't stop kicking day and night."

"And the cramping?"

"It didn't start until I got back from work. About an hour and a half ago. It's eased off now."

"Okay." Sally passed a small plastic disc over Gabby's stomach that was attached to the machine. "Let's see if we can find the little one's heartbeat." Gabby clutched Haze's hand and held her breath. For several long, tense seconds, the nurse pressed the cold monitor into different parts of Gabby's belly.

A muffled sound fluttered from the speaker. "There it is. Sounds strong."

Gabby released her breath on a sob. Haze wrapped her in an embrace and kissed her temple. Sally wrapped an elastic belt around Gabby's waist, holding the monitor in place. "We'll let this run for about half an hour. Take this and press this button if you feel any movement." Gabby took the round clicker and concentrated on listening to her baby's strong heartbeat. Alive. Her baby was alive. More tears fell. She had never been so happy and relieved in her life.

"I've never heard anything like it." Haze gazed at the numbers on the monitor, tracking the heartbeats. "It's amazing."

"I thought he was gone." Gabby's voice came out in a whimper.

"A boy?"

Gabby nodded. "I think so. He kicks like one."

"Some girls are pretty good kickers too." Haze grinned.

"True." Gabby looked away from the monitor and into Haze's eyes. "You're the first one to hear the heartbeat."

"Nikki?"

"She missed my last scan. She had to work late. Probably an excuse to be with her mistress." As she spoke another cramp gripped her. "Ow."

"You need to relax. All this stress isn't good for you."

"Not exactly the best time to be cheated on, is it?" At Haze's frown, she said, "Sorry, that wasn't necessary." Gabby looked back to the monitor as the cramp eased.

"It's okay. You're allowed to be upset. Has she tried contacting you at all?"

"No. She probably thinks this is still my own fault." She felt a small flutter, low in her belly. He kicked! She pressed the button as instructed. "How about you?"

"She texted yesterday, asking to meet up for a drink, but I ignored the message."

Gabby drew in a breath. "You know, Haze, she's still your friend. If you want to go see her, you can."

Haze shook her head. "I don't think I should."

"You've known her for thirty years. That's a lot to give up on, no matter the circumstances." Nicole may have cheated on Gabby, but she hadn't done anything to Haze, aside from some nasty words. That shouldn't be enough to throw away a friendship. Gabby wouldn't be happy about it, but Haze's friendship with Nicole was none of her business.

"You wouldn't be mad?"

"As long as she doesn't accuse us of sleeping together again, I think it would be all right." The baby kicked again. Gabby smiled. "He's waking up, I think. He's moved twice now."

"That's great."

Sally came back in with a midwife, who checked the heartbeat strip. She checked Gabby's blood pressure, then scribbled in her chart. She looked up. "Everything looks good. I'll book you in for another scan next week. If you think there is a problem before then, just come straight in. You need to think about reducing your stress levels. Your blood pressure is a little high, so we need to watch that." She glanced at Haze. "Look after her, okay?"

"I will."

After a few more instructions, and waiting another half an hour to be discharged, Haze took Gabby home. "Can I get you anything?" Haze asked, as Gabby settled under the covers of Haze's bed.

"No, I'm fine, thank you."

Haze knelt on the carpet next to her, running her fingers through Gabby's hair. Her gaze was soft and caring. "Is he still moving?"

"A few times. Perhaps he was just tired from kicking around my insides for weeks."

"I'm sure he'll be okay." Haze leaned in and kissed her forehead, her lips gentle and warm against Gabby's skin.

"Thank you, Haze, for being there with me."

Haze glanced away. "It should have been Nikki."

"Yes, it should, but I'm glad it was you. If you do see her, please don't tell her about this."

"Do you think that's fair? It's her baby too."

Trust Haze to be the honourable one in all this. As much as Gabby didn't want to see Nicole, keeping this from her wasn't fair. She had a right to know. "Damn, you're right. I'll text her in a bit and tell her."

"Give me a yell if you need anything." Haze stood and tucked her in.

"I will. Thank you."

"No problem."

CHAPTER NINE

Haze sat quietly on the sofa sketching out a few designs for the project she was working on. Her thoughts absently drifted to Gabby sleeping in the bedroom. Seeing her hunched over and clutching her stomach had scared the shit out of her. How she managed to get them to the hospital without causing an accident, she didn't know. When the sounds of the heartbeat filled the room, Haze's own heart rate had settled back to normal. She didn't know how she would have gotten Gabby through losing the baby. Gabby wasn't out of the woods yet. The midwife had warned of her stress levels. *I hope Nikki doesn't cause more problems for her. There is only so much one person can take.*

Her mobile beeped from the cushion next to her. She picked it up and saw a text from Melissa, her dance date for the evening. Haze had texted her once Gabby was settled for the night and apologised for not turning up. Melissa was understanding, and they had texted back and forth for the last hour. The flirting was fun, but Haze's heart wasn't in it. She had met Melissa at a café, a few months ago, when they interviewed for the same client. Haze won the contract. That didn't stop Melissa from asking her to stay for a coffee. They had met up twice since then. Haze knew there would never be anything between them. Melissa just wasn't her type. No, her type was tucked up in her bed.

Haze sighed. She texted back a witty reply, not sure why she was even keeping Melissa on the hook. She had only told Gabby she had a date to stop her seduction. Now Haze was stuck flirting with a woman she only thought of as a friend. She would need to end it before Melissa got even more interested.

A knock on the front door gave her a start. She looked at the time on her phone. Nine thirty. She stood from the couch and opened the door.

"Nikki, what are you doing here?"

Nikki brushed past her and glanced around the room. Her eyes were wild with fright. Haze had never seen her look so scared before. "Gabby texted me. Where is she? Are she and the baby okay?"

Haze gripped her forearms, trying to calm her down. "She's sleeping in the bedroom. They're fine, just a scare."

"Thank God." Nikki's features relaxed, then her gaze turned accusatory. "Why didn't you call me?"

"She didn't want me to."

"She's my wife. I should have been there."

"Hey look, I'm not getting involved in this. Sort it out between you. She asked me not to call you, and I respected her wishes." Haze was sick of being caught in the middle of the pair. She might be their friend, but that didn't mean she should have to put up with the back and forth. Nikki glared at her for another moment then shook her head.

"You're right, I'm sorry." She smiled. "Thank you for looking after her."

Haze shrugged. "No problem."

"And I'm sorry for the things I said the other day. I know you would never do anything to come between us. I guess it was easier to blame you two than look at my own mistakes. I apologise."

"Apology accepted. Let's just forget it." It wasn't okay. Nikki had made her feel dirty for trying to help Gabby. Despite her feelings, Haze would never cross that line, no matter how much she wanted to.

"Can I go see her?"

"Sure. I need to go out for a bit." She didn't, but she really didn't want to be there and listen to whatever Nikki said to Gabby. "Tell her I'll be back later." She grabbed her keys and jacket and headed out, no direction in mind.

†

Gabby stirred when the bed dipped and strong fingers ran through her hair, the touch familiar. She smiled at the tender way Haze touched her.

"Gabby, sweetheart?"

"Haze?" The voice didn't sound right. Haze's was much huskier, thicker with emotion, even when making small talk.

"It's Nicole."

Gabby opened her eyes. Nicole sat a few inches away, a welcoming smile on her lips. A moment of disappointment wafted through Gabby's thoughts. "What are you doing here?"

"I got here as soon as I read your message. Are you okay?" Nicole's free hand found Gabby's stomach with a protective hold. "The baby?"

"Yes, everything is fine. I need to lower my stress levels, but otherwise, all's good."

Nicole's eyes glistened with the news. "I'm sorry, Gabby. This is all my fault. I could have lost you both, all because of my selfish actions." The tears fell in earnest, and the only thing Gabby knew to do was gather her close as she cried. In all the years she had known Nicole, she had only seen her cry a handful of times. It was such a rare event that Gabby was flummoxed.

Nicole looked up from her place on Gabby's chest. "I promise to make it up to you. I want us to try again." Her voice was almost desperate. "I swear it's over with Rhea. Please come back. I'll do anything." She gripped Gabby harder. "We can be a family like we planned."

Wasn't this what Gabby wanted? For Nicole to beg for forgiveness? *Yes, but I don't want that now. I could never trust her again. How can I believe what she says?* As she stared at Nicole's hopeful expression, she heard herself say, "I can't come back to that house."

"I'll sell it. We can find somewhere else, start making happy memories again. Gabby, I love you. Please say yes."

"I don't know if I can trust you."

"I'll do anything you want." Nicole cupped her cheek. "We can take it slow. I need you…and the baby."

She looks truly heartbroken but hopeful. Could I ever take her back? What about Haze? Haze said it would never

74

happen between us. Nicole is here now. She's my wife. "It'll take time—"

Nicole's mouth covered hers. The deep kiss was so familiar, but strange. Gabby didn't feel anything. It was like kissing a stranger. Haze's face flashed in her mind and guilt swamped her. She felt like she was cheating on Haze.

"Thank you, honey." Nicole's face beamed. "You won't regret it."

I already do.

†

Haze returned home forty minutes later. She'd hoped Nikki would be gone, but her car was still parked outside. Haze debated whether to take another walk around the block. *This is my home. I shouldn't be afraid to go inside, despite what I might find on the other side of the door.*

She walked through the living room and into the kitchen. Gabby sat at the table with a cup of tea in front of her. Nikki sat close with an arm wrapped around her shoulder. She was speaking softly. Gabby's gaze was fixed on her cup. She looked stiff and uncomfortable.

"Hey guys." Haze painted on a smile. "You look cosy." She motioned to their close proximity.

Nikki grinned at Haze. "Gabby has agreed to give me another chance."

"Really?" Haze looked at Gabby, who was yet to glance up from the table. She didn't seem thrilled with the announcement but made no attempt to correct Nikki.

"Yeah. Isn't she amazing?" Nikki kissed Gabby's cheek. Gabby's eyes closed at the contact. "We're going to sell the

75

house and find somewhere else to start again. We're going to be so happy."

"That's great. I'm pleased for you both." There was no enthusiasm in her voice. How could there be? Gabby and Nikki were trying again. She couldn't begrudge them that chance, but did it have to hurt so damn much?

"Nicole, it's getting late." Gabby sounded weary. "I need to get my rest."

Nikki straightened, her features concerned. "Of course, sweetheart. I'll call you in the morning." She rose from the chair. "You're taking some time off work, I assume?"

"Yes, for a few days."

"Great." She leaned in and kissed Gabby on the lips. "I'll text you when I get home. I love you."

"Love you too."

The front door closed, and a deafening silence claimed the small kitchen. The quiet hum of the fridge rose loud in the void. Beer. Haze pushed off the archway and walked behind Gabby, feeling the gaze that tracked her every movement. Haze grabbed a beer from inside the fridge.

"Hazel…"

"What?" She twisted off the cap and tossed it into the sink. *I hate when she calls me that.*

"Talk to me."

"About what?"

"I can see you're angry."

"Of course I'm angry." Haze slammed her bottle onto the countertop, frothing beer out the top and down the sides. "A few days ago you wanted to sleep with me. You told me it was over between you two, how you didn't want to be with her. And now?" She lifted her arms in the air in an angry gesture. "Now you're setting up home together again. Do you know what? I thought Nikki was bad cheating on you, but you're worse. The minute she came back making promises, you couldn't wait to reconcile." The words were harsh. She only halfway meant them, but she was mightily pissed off. *How dare she do this to me.* They may have agreed to only be friends, but the rejection hurt, nonetheless.

"It wasn't like that." Gabby's eyes teared, as she pleaded with Haze.

"Really? I was right to turn you down. You would have used me for a quick fuck, then gone back to her anyway."

"No, I wouldn't have."

"So, if I had said yes, you would have turned her away tonight? Rode off into the sunset with me? I don't think so." Haze picked up her bottle and finished what was left in three quick swallows. "You two deserve each other." She tossed the bottle into the recycling.

"I didn't know what to say. She came in all upset and begging for forgiveness. I didn't have it in me to say no." Gabby stood and approached Haze, who now leaned against the counter. "When she kissed me, I felt nothing. I've felt more from the way you look at me." She reached out, but Haze pushed her hand away. "Haze, I don't know what to do. I can't raise this baby on my own."

"So you'd rather go back to a cheater?"

"I don't know. I'm so confused." She stepped closer, trapping Haze. Gabby's gaze dropped to her lips. "I can't stop thinking about you, but she's my wife. I have to try, don't I?"

Gabby looked so torn, unsure of the right thing to do. If it was up to Haze, she would tell Nikki where to go and have Gabby all to herself. But it wasn't up to her. "Only you can decide that, Gabby." She stepped around her and distanced herself from the battle. Having Gabby so close was lessening her resolve. She couldn't give in, not when Nicole was set on having Gabby back. "I'll tell you one thing. I'm not going to sit around waiting for you to choose. I changed my date to next Friday, and I intend to go." She didn't feel triumphant at the sight of Gabby's head lowered in defeat. "I'm done pining for you." She walked away and slammed into her office. She had no claim on Gabby. Gabby was free to do as she pleased. If Gabby wasn't strong enough to say no to Nikki, who was Haze to decide for her? She made her bed, now she can lie in it. *Don't come crying to me when she rips your heart out again. Like you did to me.*

CHAPTER TEN

Haze threaded the brown, leather belt through the loops on her jeans and and buckled the bronze clasp. She slipped her feet into her boots, then straightened to look at herself in the mirror. Not bad. She wasn't looking forward to her date with Melissa. She wanted to hide away in her office like she had done all week. Hiding from everyone was one perk of working from home. She could shut the world away and work without having to see anybody. Avoiding Gabby had been difficult. Haze would greet Gabby when she came home from school, then escape to her office, where she stayed all night until she knew Gabby had gone to bed. Only then would Haze venture out and get something quick to eat and make up the couch to sleep on. As far as Haze knew, Gabby was still set on reconciling with Nikki. She didn't know why.

Anyone could see Gabby wasn't into it. *Maybe if I were an option Gabby would change her mind.* It was a stupid thought. If Gabby didn't want to be with Nikki, then she should tell her. Having Haze as a backup wasn't the way to choose. As much as Haze wanted to be with Gabby, Gabby would need to make the choice. Haze wouldn't push her. *If she can so easily go back to Nikki, do I really want to be with her anyway? It's all too messed up. Better to just go out tonight and have a good time. You never know, Melissa might just catch my interest.* She doubted it, but hiding away and mooning over Gabby wasn't going to help Haze move on with her life. Gabby and Nikki belonged together. Haze would only ever be their friend.

She took one last look in the mirror, then headed to the kitchen for a beer to settle her nerves. Gabby sat at the table, marking assignments. Her hair was loose, tumbling over one shoulder. Haze saw her lips purse, as she wrote on someone's homework, and moved toward the fridge to avoid Gabby's guarded glance in her direction.

"Hey," Gabby greeted her.

"Hi." Haze closed the door, then found a glass. She poured the amber liquid slowly, without forming a head. "How are you feeling?"

"Tired. Edith has been great, letting me do half days all week. She thinks I should take early maternity leave. Nicole does too."

Haze took a swig and really looked at Gabby. Circles still smudged her eyes. The fine lines at her temples seemed deeper than usual. She was still beautiful but looked exhausted. "Might be a good idea." She sat opposite Gabby, placing her glass on the table where no papers rested. Gabby gazed at her from under lowered lashes. She seemed nervous.

"Are things going okay between you two?" Haze asked, alluding to Nikki.

Gabby shrugged. "She's saying all the right things. Even contacted an estate agent about selling the house." She glanced away, her brows pinching.

"But?"

"But nothing. Everything has gone back to normal. Well, as normal as it can be living apart."

"So, you're still set on reconciliation?" *I really am a glutton for punishment.* She didn't want to know about their relationship, not anymore. Everything had changed when Gabby showed up two weeks ago, asking for a place to stay. Haze would never make Gabby leave before she was ready, but having her go back to Nikki after expressing a romantic interest was heartbreaking. It was so much easier when Haze could avoid them and keep her love for Gabby to herself.

"I don't know. When we went out Wednesday evening, I found it strained. I didn't know what to say to her. She made up for the lack of conversation on my part by talking about the new merger at her work. I couldn't tell you what she said. I wasn't listening. All I could see was her in bed with someone else." She stared intently at Haze. "I don't think it's going to work."

"Then you need to tell her, before she finds you a nice house with a white picket fence and a puppy."

Gabby's eyes narrowed. "Why are you being so mean?"

"I can't help it." What was she supposed to do? Get up on the table and jump for joy? "I'm sorry." She finished off her beer and swilled out the glass at the sink. She left it upside down to drain.

81

"You look very nice." Gabby was looking her up and down. Haze's skin warmed under the perusal. "Where are you taking her?"

"To that new Italian place in town."

"That's supposed to be very good."

"Hopefully."

"I'll see you when you get back?"

Haze shook her head and walked past the table toward the living room. "Don't wait up. We might go dancing later."

"Oh, okay. Haze?"

"Yeah?" Haze turned and raised her eyebrows in question.

Gabby took a breath, then stuttered, "Have …a nice time."

"Thanks." Haze was sure Gabby meant to say something else but refrained from asking.

Two hours later, she was leading Melissa through the door of the club. Dinner conversation had flowed easily between them. Under any other circumstances, Haze might be tempted to date Melissa. *She isn't Gabby.* Melissa was short, while Gabby nearly matched Haze's five foot nine. Melissa's short, blonde bob didn't compare to Gabby's soft brown curls. Haze could get lost in the depths of Gabby's chocolate-coloured eyes, while Melissa's blue just didn't captivate her. Melissa was pretty, for sure, but she didn't get Haze going the way Gabby did.

I need to get Gabby out of my head, for God's sake. I'm on a date. Act like it.

"Are you sure you want to do this?" Melissa asked as they headed out onto the dance floor. "You don't seem that into it."

"Of course I do. I promised you dancing, so let's dance."

Haze threaded her arms around Melissa's waist, Melissa's going around her neck. Haze pulled her in close and inserted a thigh between Melissa's. They ground their bodies in time to the beat. Haze forced her eyes to stay open, to focus on Melissa. If she closed them, she knew she would see Gabby in her arms.

"You know," Melissa whispered, "you're very sexy when you dance like that."

"Oh yeah?" Haze grinned, pulled her closer, and nibbled her ear. *What the hell am I doing?* "How about now?"

"Even better." Melissa groaned. "Why don't we go somewhere else, and you can show me what other moves you have?"

Haze gazed into Melissa's eyes, willing herself to feel anything for her, but there was nothing. There was no doubt in her mind Melissa wouldn't be the one. It was time to leave, take Melissa home, and go back to her own place, alone.

"I'd like that." *What the hell. I need a release, and at least Melissa wants me.* She knew she'd regret it in the morning, but that was tomorrow's problem.

†

Gabby checked the time on her phone for the tenth time that hour. Haze still wasn't home. It was coming up to eleven thirty. *By the looks of things, Haze isn't coming back tonight.* It shouldn't bother Gabby. Haze was free to see whomever she wanted. If she wanted to stay out all night, that was her prerogative too. That didn't stop Gabby feeling jealous. She had no claim on Haze. *Besides, I'm supposed to be getting back on track with Nicole. What Haze does and who she does it with are none of my business.*

She tossed the duvet aside and rose from the bed, taking her phone with her to the kitchen. She grabbed a saucepan, then the jug from the fridge, and set about making some warm milk. *Hopefully, this will help me sleep.* She stirred the milk to stop it burning to the pan. *Her thoughts seem to swirl with the milk.* Nicole hadn't turned up for the scan the doctors had arranged, claiming work was too busy. Gabby had tried to not let her suspicions get the better of her, but it was hard. How many times had Nicole used that excuse before sneaking off to meet her lover? On the other hand, Nicole had looked so devastated when she had turned up begging for forgiveness last week. Would she really be so stupid to carry on an affair? No answers were forthcoming.

Gabby poured the warm milk into a mug and wandered into the lounge. She peeked through the blinds, hoping to see Haze's car pull up. The streets were dark. No sign of movement from anyone. Gabby turned her back on the window and placed her mug on the coffee table. She didn't want to sit there waiting up for her all night. Imagining Haze in bed with another woman would drive her crazy. *It already is. She obviously likes this woman and wants her, not you.* Gabby knew Haze had feelings for her but was determined to run from them. She couldn't blame Haze. *I guess I'd better start giving Nicole a proper chance. If Haze can have a night of wild sex, why can't I?* Going against her better judgment, she grabbed her phone from the kitchen table and rang Nicole.

"Nicole, it's Gabby. I know it's late, but can you meet me somewhere?"

"Gabby? What? Why?" Nicole's reply was raspy. No doubt Gabby had woken her up.

"I need to see you, but I can't come to the house."

"I could come to Haze's."

"No!" How awful would that be if Haze came home and found Nicole in bed with Gabby? Gabby would never disrespect Haze's home like that. "Please. Let's find a hotel." Nicole was silent for so long, Gabby thought she'd refuse.

"Gabby, are you sure?"

No. "Yes. I need to see you. Now."

They agreed on a place to meet, then Gabby hung up. She rushed into the bedroom to get ready. She tried to conjure up a time when she was madly in love with Nicole and their sex life was active. She needed to get her head and heart switched on to the thing she was about to do. She tried to tell herself it would be the perfect way to reconnect with Nicole, to bring the passion back into their relationship. Deep down, she knew she was using Nicole as a distraction to take her mind off Haze being with another woman. *This is a mistake, but I'm committed to it now. Nicole was her wife. Haze was a friend. Everything was as it should be.*

Two hours later, Nicole rolled away from Gabby, panting hard, sweat slicking her skin. "Wow. That was intense."

Gabby closed her eyes, trapping the tears inside. The sex had been pleasant enough. Nicole always knew the right places to touch to elicit a response from her, and yes, they had both orgasmed. But it wasn't Nicole Gabby had been thinking of as Nicole's hand and mouth brought her to the edge. It was Haze. For the first time in her life, Gabby had been thinking of someone else while in bed with her wife.

"It was great," Gabby replied with as much enthusiasm as she could muster. Nicole's hand found her breast, teasing her nipple. Gabby screwed her eyes shut.

"Ready to go again?" Nicole's breath was warm on her neck.

"It's late. I should think about getting home."

"We've booked the whole night. Why don't we stay?" Nicole's hand slipped lower, inching towards Gabby's thighs.

"I really can't. I have to be up early to go to school for a staff meeting."

"On a Saturday?"

"Yeah. I can't miss it." Gabby sat up and looked about for her clothes. She felt dirty. The minute she was home, she would be showering. Never before had being with Nicole made her feel so cheap, but it did. She didn't know if it was because Nicole had cheated or because Gabby's feelings for Haze were clouding her mind. She wanted to go home. She wanted to erase this night from her memory.

"Oh, okay."

Gabby dressed silently, not looking at Nicole.

"Gabby?"

"Yeah?"

"Are we okay?"

Gabby's movements stilled. Now would be the time to be honest. To tell her no, they weren't okay. She glanced at Nicole, seeing the worry and confusion in her gaze. "We're fine. I guess I'm still struggling with everything." That part was true. Nicole didn't need to know about Haze.

"I understand, but I assume the fact we just made love is a good sign?"

Made love? We had sex. Nothing more, nothing less. "Yes. I have to go." She slipped her coat on and grabbed her keys. Nicole still sat on the bed, looking lost. "I'll call you tomorrow." She leaned down and kissed Nicole's cheek, then strode from the room without giving Nicole a chance to stop her leaving. *What have I done?*

CHAPTER ELEVEN

Gabby pulled up outside Haze's house, her heart pounding. Haze's car was in the driveway. Did that mean Haze had brought her date home? Were they in there now having sex? No, she wouldn't do that. If Haze was going to spend the night with someone, she would go to their place. Gabby stepped from the car and headed inside. Haze shot up from the couch and rushed toward her, grabbing her arms.

"Are you okay? I've been worried sick something happened to you."

"What? I'm fine." Haze's eyes were wild, and Gabby could see her pulse hammering in her neck. "I thought you were out all night?" She stepped around Haze, hoping she couldn't smell the lingering scent of sex clinging to her skin.

"I came home an hour ago. I saw the mug of milk on the coffee table and your phone in the kitchen. I thought something had happened with the baby."

Gabby closed her eyes, her back to Haze. Guilt swamped her and flushed out the truth. "I was with Nicole." She walked to the kitchen, and heard Haze trailing behind her. "I'm sorry you were worried. How did your night go?" She tried to keep her tone light, hoping Haze wouldn't question her further. She grabbed a water from the fridge and took three large gulps, glancing at Haze as she did so. She looked hurt.

"It was nice, but I don't think I'll be seeing her again."

"How come?"

Haze shrugged. "Not my type. She invited me back to her place. Once I got there, I couldn't go through with it." She shrugged again, her eyes narrowing. "You were with Nicole?"

Gabby dropped into a kitchen chair, head resting in her hands. She was right, she had made the biggest mistake of her life. She had slept with Nicole, because she thought Haze was having sex with someone else. But she wasn't. She had come home. Gabby lifted her head. A tear rolled down her cheek as she nodded. "I slept with her."

"Oh." Haze frowned. "That's good, though. Means you're moving in the right direction with her."

"No. That's not what it means." Gabby rose and moved within touching distance of Haze. "I slept with her, because I was jealous that you were out with someone else. I thought you were making love to your date, and I couldn't stand it. I phoned Nicole, because I couldn't sit here waiting for you to come back." She took a breath. "The whole time I was with her, I was thinking of you." She reached out, grasping Haze's hands. "I don't want to be with her, Haze. I want to be with you."

Haze shook her head. "No, Gabby. You belong with Nikki. You love Nikki."

"I don't. Not anymore."

"It's only been a few weeks. You can't possibly want me."

"But I do. Please, Haze. Just give us a chance."

Haze stepped back, releasing Gabby's hands. Her whole body trembled. "We can't do this, Gabby. Nikki is my friend. Despite what she has done, it wouldn't be fair."

"Haze—"

"No. You can't sleep with her, then tell me you want to be with me. You keep changing your mind. I don't think you have any idea who you want."

Gabby glared at Haze, her heart beating wildly. *How dare she assume she knows what I'm feeling.* She stepped closer. "Since the moment I met you, I've been attracted to you. You know this. Moving in here and seeing you every day has strengthened my feelings for you."

"But you took Nikki back."

"I told you, that's because I didn't know how to turn her down."

"And have you? Told her that you no longer love her?"

Gabby looked down at the carpet, her cheeks heating. Haze laughed. "See? You haven't even told her, and you expect me to swoop you up and be with you. We're going round in circles. You're keeping us both on the hook, and I'm not putting up with it." Haze relaxed her features. Her smile seemed so sad. "I don't think you being here is going to work."

"What?"

"I'm sorry. I know I promised you could stay here as long as you wanted, but it's too hard."

Gabby stared at Haze as her words sunk in. She was kicking her out. *I can't go home.* But Haze was right. It wasn't working. *Am I confused about what I want?* She continued to stare at Haze. *No. I know what I want and it's Haze. But Haze won't accept it.* Gabby hung her head, defeated. She would need to leave.

"I don't want you to go, believe me, but it's for the best."

"You're right. I'll call my mother, see if I can stay with them for a while."

"What about Nikki?"

"She'll understand." She hoped. "I'm sorry about all this." She stepped around Haze and avoided looking at her. Gabby was embarrassed to have put herself out there and been shot down. How mortifying! Maybe getting away for a while would be for the best.

"Gabby?"

Gabby glanced over her shoulder, holding her tears back. She wouldn't let Haze see her break down.

"I really am sorry."

"No problem." Gabby tried to smile with the use of Haze's favourite phrase. She walked to the bedroom, shut the door, and curled up on the bed. I'm an idiot.

†

Gabby was in the last twenty minutes of the drive to her parents' house in Hammersmith. She had been on the road since five that morning, wanting to leave before Haze woke up. Gabby had been humiliated the night before. Not only had she made the mistake of sleeping with Nicole, but she

91

had also thrown herself at Haze. Being shot down was never a pleasant feeling. Having it come from Haze was worse. *How can I make her see I'm serious?* Gabby had also taken the coward's way out with Nicole. She sent her a text, telling her she needed time away to think things through. *Is Haze right? Am I keeping them both on the hook?* Gabby didn't know why she couldn't tell Nicole it was over. She would never be able to forgive her for cheating. *Even if I weren't attracted to Haze, I still wouldn't be able to go back to Nicole. Then why not just tell her?*

She pulled into her mother's driveway. The house was always the same. The gardener kept the lawn and hedges neatly trimmed, and bright-white walls were recently painted. The five bedroom house had been the Carter's family home since Gabby could remember. Her father worked in finance. Her mother was a teacher, like Gabby

Gabby had never wanted for anything growing up, but her father always worked. Claire Carter was left to raise Gabby and her sister, to make sure they were clean and always had food on the table. The housekeeper helped a lot but Gabby knew her mother had made her into the woman she was today.

She heaved herself from the car, then went up the pathway to the front door. After a few minutes, Claire answered the knock. She wore her pink dressing gown, her greying hair in rollers.

"Gabriella? What are you doing here?"

Gabby tried to smile, but it came off as a grimace. She tilted her head down, as tears burst from her eyes. "Everything has gone wrong."

"Oh, sweetheart." Claire reached out pulled her into a hug. "Come here." She allowed Gabby to cry for a moment. "Go into the lounge, and I'll make us some tea."

Gabby followed her mother through the wide hall and toward the lounge. As her mother left the room, Gabby settled on the newly purchased black-leather couch and pulled the blanket off the back. She wrapped the throw around herself, resting one hand on her belly. The baby hadn't been shy about letting Gabby know he was displeased at sitting in a car for nearly three hours. He had been kicking her insides like crazy. He was still now, probably glad to be nestled on a comfy chair instead of being jostled about in the cramped car.

The china teapot and cups Claire carried into the room barely rattled. She carefully settled the tray onto the oak coffee table in front of Gabby. "Where's Dad?"

"Casino with his buddies." Claire frowned. "Where else?" She poured the tea but left the cups on the table as she sat next to Gabby.

"Why do you put up with that?" It was eight in the morning. No doubt her father had been out all night.

"Honey, relationships are complicated. I love him, and he loves me. He knows he has a problem, and we're working through it." Claire smiled, turning her wedding ring on her finger. "I can't give up on him just because he has an addiction."

Is that what I should do with Nicole? Give her a chance to fix things?

"Now. What brought you here so early in the morning? Is my grandbaby okay?"

"He's fine." Gabby took a breath and looked everywhere except at her mother. She struggled to find the words that

93

could explain everything. Her parents had always loved Nicole, treated her as their daughter. They would be devastated to learn what she had done. Gabby finally focused, when she felt Claire's hand touch her knee on top of the blanket. "A few weeks ago, I came home and found Nicole sleeping with someone else."

Claire's eyes went wide, her forehead creasing. "Oh."

"It's been going on for months. I've been staying at Haze's, and now I'm all confused."

"About what, honey?"

About what I want. "I think I'm in love with her."

"Well, of course. You married her."

Gabby shook her head. "No, not Nicole. Haze."

"That would complicate things, wouldn't it?" Claire paused for a moment, pursing her lips. She always had a lot of patience, taking time to think things through before speaking. That trait made her a great teacher. "Why do you think you love Hazel?"

"We've always been attracted to each other. But I was with Nicole and that attraction went away. Or so I thought. These last couple of weeks, my feelings have come back. I know Haze wants me too, but she won't do anything about it because of Nicole."

"And what about Nicole?"

"She wants me back, but I don't think I can be with her anymore. She broke my heart. Haze thinks I'm just angry at Nicole and don't know what I want. But when I look at her, it's like a million sparks go zipping through my body. My stomach flips, and I forget my voice for a second." Gabby felt her skin flush at the images that rolled through her mind. She shrugged the blanket off, needing to cool down. "I never had that with Nicole. It was comfortable. We had plans. With

Haze, life feels exciting, like I always imagined being in love would be." She had thought she held those feelings for Nicole. In hindsight, maybe she had been pretending. With Haze, there was a burning desire in the pit of her stomach that she never had for her wife. *Am I a bad person?*

"If you hadn't have caught Nicole with someone else, would you still be together?"

Gabby gave the question some serious thought. She thought over their life together, and the life that was growing inside her now. Her attraction to Haze might have always been there, but she never would have questioned her relationship with Nicole if she hadn't caught her having sex with someone else.

"Yes."

"So, perhaps Hazel is right, and you're still upset by the betrayal. Maybe you're transferring your anger into feelings for Hazel that aren't really there."

Gabby drew her brows down. "I... I don't think so."

"But you're not sure?"

This is such a mess. "What am I going to do?"

"You don't need to figure it out now." Claire lifted her arm, and Gabby curled into her mother, resting her head on her chest as she always did when growing up. "You can stay here as long as you need, you know that. It'll give us time to catch up properly."

"I don't really want to be here if things with Dad are strained."

"We're fine. He'd love to see you too."

"Thanks, Mum."

"Anytime, sweetheart."

Claire began humming. The soft tones gently lulled Gabby to sleep. Images of Haze and Nicole wrapped around her mind. Her confusion over everything had gained momentum, and she realised it would take more than a few days to find any clear answers. One thing she did know, she missed Haze like crazy, and it had only been a few hours since she had seen her last.

CHAPTER TWELVE

Haze sat across from Nikki in one of the local pubs. For a Friday evening, it was pretty quiet. Haze would have preferred it a little noisier to limit their conversation. It was getting harder to face Nikki. Although Haze hadn't crossed a line with Gabby, they were both thinking about it. If she had slept with Gabby, there was no doubt in Haze's mind she wouldn't be sitting here. She had seen Nikki only once since Gabby left. The day she left. According to Nikki, Gabby had texted her saying she needed time to think. Haze couldn't bring herself to tell Nikki that she had asked Gabby to leave.

"It's been nearly a month." Nikki wrapped her hand in a tight grip around the wine glass. "Are you sure you haven't heard from her?"

"No." Haze shook her head and sipped her beer. "I haven't." Haze had only received a message the week Gabby left. She had apologised about her behaviour and said she never meant to hurt anyone. Aside from that, there had been no contact, not even a reply to Haze's text asking if she was alright. *Maybe she's gone for good.* The thought didn't bear thinking about. Haze would never get over not seeing Gabby again. She assumed Nikki thought the same, considering her forlorn expression.

"You still haven't told me why she left."

"She told you. She said she needed time away to think." At least that's partly true.

"About what? Last time I saw her, we had just had the best sex in forever. She said we were fine. Why would she leave?"

This was getting unbearable. There was only so long Haze would be able to keep the truth to herself. If Nikki didn't stop asking questions, Haze would be forced to reveal everything that had happened since Nikki was caught cheating. If Nikki knew just how close Haze and Gabby had come to sleeping with each other, that would be the end of their friendship. *Not that keeping it quiet is helping. I can hardly look at her.*

"Nikki, I don't know. Whatever goes on between you, is between you guys. I don't know anything."

Nikki narrowed her eyes, forcing Haze to look away. "So nothing happened between you two?"

Haze's gaze flew back to Nikki. "Are you serious? Yes, Nikki. We were fucking all around the house. Having a great laugh about you. Is that what you want to hear?" Haze's voice had risen, and a couple on the next table turned to glare at them.

"I'm sorry. I just don't understand how she could leave."

Because fucking is what we wanted to do, but I couldn't do that to you. Besides, I don't know if she truly wants me. The whole situation was driving her crazy. "Give her some time. She'll come back when she's ready."

"I wonder if everything is okay with the baby."

"I'm sure she'd tell you if there was a problem."

"I doubt it. I haven't exactly been a good parent so far. I promised I'd do everything right if she gave me another chance, but I didn't even make it to the scan."

"Are you kidding me? Even after the scare she had?" Nikki had the good grace to blush. "She could have done with your support." *Why didn't she tell me Nikki never showed up? I could have been there for her.*

"I know. I messed up."

"You keep making a habit of that. What was your excuse?"

"I had to work. We're close to finalising the merger, and I had to go to a meeting with the company director."

"Really?" Haze hoped that was true, because if Nikki was still cheating on Gabby, then screw their friendship. Haze wouldn't tolerate Gabby being hurt anymore. She gazed intently into Nikki's eyes, looking for the lie. Thankfully, she saw only honesty from her.

"Yes, really. I told you, it's over with Rhea."

"Do you think Gabby believes that?"

"Probably not. But how can I prove it to her if she isn't here?"

"As I said. Give her time." Haze was done talking about Gabby. Her heart hurt, her house felt barren without Gabby's presence, and all this talking was making Haze miss her more. Thankfully, Nikki changed the subject.

"Anyway, how are things with you?"

"Work is going great." She took another swig of her drink. "I picked up two new clients."

"What about your love life?"

Haze frowned. "There isn't one."

"Didn't you have a date a while back?"

"Yeah. She was nice enough but didn't really do anything for me."

Nikki stared at her for a long moment, chewing the inside of her cheek. "Haze, you're going to have to let go of Gabby eventually."

Haze's temper flared, ready to have a go at Nikki for bringing her up again. She looked at her friend and saw only concern. "I know."

Nikki reached across the table, stilling Haze's hand as she twirled her glass in circles on the scarred wood table. "You really do love her, don't you?"

"You know I would never do anything."

"It doesn't matter. She loves me. We're married and having a kid. Once this all blows over, we'll be back together. You're my best friend. I don't want to see you lonely for the rest of your life."

Haze looked up from under her lashes. "You confuse me."

"How so?" Nikki pulled back her hand.

"One minute you're accusing us of having an affair, and the next you're talking like you don't mind I have feelings for her."

Nikki let out a big sigh and shook her head. "This has all been one big mess, hasn't it? I guess, on the one hand, I see you as a threat—a woman who loves my wife. On the other, you're Haze, my best friend. I know you would never do

100

anything to hurt me. We've all been together for ten years. I'm learning to accept things. You need to, too. I know she had an attraction to you, but I also know she loves me." She smirked. "We did get married, after all."

Haze couldn't help but think that was Nikki's way of one-upping her. As if Haze didn't know Gabby belonged to Nikki. She always knew that. It didn't stop her feelings, though. If Gabby did go back to Nikki, Haze would live with it, like she always had.

"Whatever happens, one, if not all of us, will end up hurt," Haze said. *More than likely me.*

"Yes. If she doesn't come back, I will have lost my wife. If she does, you'll still be loving from afar."

Not if she chooses me. Then you'll be hurt. "I guess it's down to Gabby to decide if she's coming back or not." And who she wants to be with, if either of us.

"But you'll always be my best friend?"

"Of course." Haze put as much enthusiasm into her voice as she could muster. Deep down, she had a feeling that after the dust settled, Nikki wouldn't be in her life. Maybe, not even Gabby.

†

Gabby walked into the dining room, finding her father sat at the table with his laptop. She pulled out a chair and sat adjacent to him. "Hey, Dad." Mitchell Carter's bushy eyebrows overlapped the top of his glasses. He was aging well; only a few lines marred his features, but his eyebrows were always out of control. They were grey now, instead of the jet black they once were.

"Hi, Gabby. You okay?"

101

"Yeah." Gabby rubbed between her breasts. "I've got major acid reflux, though." The last few weeks, she hadn't been able to tolerate some foods, onions being one of them. Not realising, Claire had cooked Gabby an omelet. Gabby ate the breakfast, not wanting to be rude. She regretted that decision now. Mitchell beamed, glancing at her bump.

"Not long until my grandchild shows up."

"Just over seven weeks." And it couldn't come soon enough. Her feet were swollen. She couldn't get comfortable when she slept, and her maternity trousers were getting larger. Not only that, but she was peeing nonstop. To say she was anxious to get the baby out would be an understatement.

"Are you looking forward to being a mum?"

"I'm excited to meet the little guy, but besides that..." Her shoulders slumped. "How can I bring a baby into the world, when I don't even have anywhere to live?"

"Why don't you consider moving back here permanently? I'm sure your mother would love the chance to help look after the baby."

"I can't." That would be a nightmare for Gabby. She loved her mother but knew if she stayed there, her mother would end up taking over. It wasn't that Claire thought Gabby couldn't cope. She was just a hoverer. Gabby wouldn't be able to learn without thinking she was doing everything wrong. "I have a job and friends back in Bristol. It's my home." Edith had been fine about Gabby taking early maternity leave, although Gabby didn't tell her the real reason why. She felt bad for lying, blaming high blood pressure. She wasn't up to divulging the ugly state of her relationship and her need to get away from Haze.

"Any chance you and Nicole can work things out? I know she cheated on you, but we all make mistakes."

Mitchell looked away with heated cheeks, as he said the words. Gabby narrowed her eyes. "You cheated on Mum?"

He nodded, still not looking at her. "Only once. With her friend." He looked at Gabby, shame on his face. "We were drunk, and I made a very stupid mistake. Your mother forgave me, and I've spent every day since being the best husband I can be."

"Really? The best husband you can be?" Gabby didn't mean to sound so sarcastic, but how could he think he was the best husband? He always worked, and was never home. Gabby couldn't even remember a time when the whole family sat down for dinner together.

"What is that supposed to mean? I worked my ass off to provide for her, to make her feel special. I never forgot one birthday, one anniversary. I tell her every day how much I love her."

I guess being a kid, I never noticed how things were between them. Perhaps I'm being too hard on him. "What about your gambling?"

Mitchell frowned, pulling his bushy eyebrows further over his glasses. "That's none of your business."

"It is if you end up spending all your money and she ends up homeless."

"Claire is supporting me in my problem." He tapped a few keys on his laptop, then turned it toward Gabby so she could see the screen. "Look."

"What's GamStop?"

He turned the screen back to face him. "It's a software program that stops you from gambling on all your devices. It blocks your details from being used on pretty much every gambling site."

"That's good, but what about the casinos?"

"That one is harder to crack." He smiled sardonically. "Claire wants me to go to a gamblers anonymous group. I'm not sure if I'm up to that yet." Mitchell turned in his chair, so he faced Gabby head on. He took one of her hands in his own. "Gabby, honey. I really do love your mother. She's the best thing that ever happened to me. I'm trying to change, and her support means the world. It would be nice if I had your support too."

"Of course I support you, Dad. I want you both to be happy."

"And that's all we want for you. I made a mistake with your mother's friend, and I was lucky she forgave me. Maybe you should do the same with Nicole." He gestured to her belly. "Then you'll have someone to help with the baby."

Gabby shook her head. "I won't go back to her just so I won't be alone. I have to trust her again, and I don't think I can do that."

He glanced at her sideways then cleared his throat. "Your mother tells me you think you might like someone else. Your friend, Hazel, isn't it?"

"Yeah."

"How does she feel about the baby?"

"Can't wait to meet him." She felt him kick beneath her hand, and she smiled. He really does have strong legs.

"And is she willing to be a mother to him?"

Gabby shook her head. "Nicole is his mother, whether we're together or not. It's her egg I'm carrying." They had decided they both wanted to be linked to the baby. Nicole had no desire to carry a child, so it was agreed Gabby would carry Nicole's egg. "Haze would make an excellent step-mum though." Her skin flushed, as she envisioned Haze holding the baby and gazing lovingly at him. It was an image she couldn't wait to make a reality. *I have to talk to her. It's driving me crazy not seeing her.*

"You really like her, don't you?"

"Yes."

"Then maybe you should tell Nicole it's over," he said carefully.

"I'm not sure how. We were together for so long. I loved her so much." Gabby's eyes teared. Not because she still loved Nicole, but because all her plans for the future were now in ruins.

"Sweetheart, dragging it out will only make things worse. If you really think you don't love her anymore, you need to tell her."

"This looks serious." Claire strolled into the room. She squeezed Gabby's shoulder as she passed, then sat next to her husband. "Anything I can help with?"

Mitchell smiled at Claire. "I was just giving our daughter love advice."

"You should listen to him." Claire beamed. "He knows what he's talking about."

The obvious affection between them warmed Gabby's heart, and she realised she really didn't know what it was like for them when she was growing up. "Can I ask you a question, Mum?"

"Of course."

"It's about Dad cheating on you."

Claire's gaze cut to her husband who lowered his head to avoid her glare. "You told her?"

He shrugged. "Seemed apropos."

Claire turned back to Gabby and blew out a breath. "What's your question?"

"Why did you forgive Dad? After what he did."

"I've been with your father for over forty years. He made a humongous error in judgment." She shook her head. "It wasn't easy, and boy did I let him have it. He cried when he told me." She looked back at Mitchell. "I'd never seen him so distraught. We took some time apart, but I couldn't stop loving him. After I came back, we had you and your sister, and things have been great ever since." She cupped his cheek, as they gazed into each other's eyes. "It took a while for the trust to come back, but I'm glad I stuck it out. He's the love of my life." Claire leaned in and kissed him quickly, then turned back to Gabby. "Does that help?"

"I haven't told you this. When I confronted Nicole, she denied it. She tried to blame it on my hormones making me see things. Then she blamed my attraction to Hazel for her reasoning to cheat. She felt lonely, like I wasn't trying anymore in the relationship."

"She knows you like Hazel?" Mitchell asked.

"It's never been a secret Haze had feelings for me. I have always had a crush on her, but I thought Nicole couldn't see it." She looked away, out the dining room windows. "I can't help thinking maybe this is all my fault."

"That's a load of crap." Anger coloured Mitchell's tone. "If she felt you were drifting apart, she should have spoken to you, not screwed someone else."

"Mitchell!"

"It's okay." Gabby smiled at her dad's defense of her. "He's right. Haze and I have never done anything. It wasn't until I moved into her place that my attraction to her grew. I can't stop thinking about her."

"Haze?"

"Yes. If I loved Nicole, shouldn't I be thinking about her?"

"All I know is, Mitchell is the only man I have thought about in that way."

"For me too," he agreed. "Your mother owns my heart. Despite my indiscretion, it's only ever been her."

"I have to break it off with Nicole, don't I? If Haze wasn't in the picture, I'd still not want to go back to Nicole. It's over." Of that she was certain. Sleeping with her again the other week was further proof it was over. Never before had she felt so dirty being with someone. All she could think about was Nicole's hands on someone else. Not only that, Haze kept intruding in on her thoughts. It was true, things with Nicole would never work. *Now all I have to do is tell her.* She would give it a few hours, then try calling her. There was no sense in putting it off much longer.

CHAPTER THIRTEEN

"Are you sure this design will work?"

Haze looked up from her laptop and smiled at her new client. They were meeting in the hotel bar, where Sandy Fisher was staying purely for this meeting with Haze. Sandy owned an art gallery up north and had contacted Haze through a mutual acquaintance, one Haze had worked for before. Sandy was so impressed with Haze's work he couldn't wait to work with her. Haze was immensely proud she had managed to land such an affluent client. *Hopefully, I'll start making some real money.*

"Definitely." She turned the laptop so Sandy could see the template. "The thumbnails of several different pieces allow you to draw a wider audience. Much better than centering on single image that might not appeal to every buyer."

"I just don't want the page to be too muddled."

"It won't be. I'll make them..." A familiar figure cut across Haze's peripheral vision. She turned her head in time to see Nicole heading into the bar, her arm wrapped tightly around a short, blonde woman. They laughed together, and to Haze, they seemed more than friends. *Please don't tell me that's Rhea.*

"Make them what?" Sandy asked. "Ms. Evens?"

"Huh?" Haze looked back to him and blinked. "Sorry. Can you excuse me for a moment?" She didn't give her client a chance to reply, as she stood and sprinted after the loved-up couple. "Nikki?"

Nikki swung around, her arm dropping from the woman's waist, her eyes wide. "Haze! Hey." She took a step away from the blonde. "What are you doing here?"

"Meeting a client." She nodded her head to the table she shared with Sandy. "What about you?"

"Um, same." She glanced at Rhea, who seemed confused by Nicole's withdrawal. "We were just on our way to the conference room."

"And who's we?"

Nikki rubbed the back of her neck and blushed. "Uh, this is Rhea. She moved back down to my department."

Haze folded her arms across her chest and glared at her. It was obvious Nikki was still cheating on Gabby. They were both dressed too casually to be going to a business meeting. They also didn't carry any bags or folders. Haze couldn't believe, after everything Nikki had promised, she could still carry on with Rhea. "Can I have a word?"

"Sure." Nikki turned to Rhea. "You go ahead. I'll be right there."

Rhea shrugged and walked away toward the bar. Haze waited for her to get out of earshot. "What the hell, Nikki?"

"It's not what it looks like."

"Really? Because it kinda looks like you're hooking up with her in a hotel."

Nikki lifted her arms, palms forward in a placating manner. "I swear, Haze. I'm not. Please, you have to believe me. If Gabby finds out Rhea is back on my team, she'll never come home."

"I wish I could believe nothing is going on, but you were all over each other."

"Gabby still isn't taking my calls." Nikki glanced down to the plush carpet. "What am I supposed to do?"

Is she serious? "I don't know, how about not screwing someone else because you're lonely? How about taking a trip to see Gabby, show her you love her?" *I can't believe I ever felt guilty for wanting to be with Gabby.*

"Look, it's no big deal. Just sex."

Haze had to rein in her temper. She was aware of Sandy watching from across the room. She didn't want to give him the impression she was unprofessional, no matter how much she wanted to wipe the smirk off Nikki's face. "Gabby is eight months pregnant and alone. How selfish can you get?"

"Please don't tell her."

"I couldn't even if I wanted to. She isn't taking my calls either. Don't look so relieved."

"Nicole?" Rhea had reappeared, without Haze noticing, and rested her hand on Nikki's back. Nikki didn't move away from her touch.

"I have to go." Nikki said to Haze.

"Think very carefully about what you're doing." Haze watched Nikki smile and turn Rhea toward the bar.

If their friendship wasn't over before, it certainly was now. Haze wouldn't stand idly by and watch Nikki carry on with another woman, whether she was with Gabby or not. She closed her eyes briefly then headed back to Sandy.

"I'm ever so sorry. Can we reschedule?" She closed her laptop and shoved it into her bag, followed by the sketches she had brought of the mocked-up website. "I have an emergency I need to attend to."

"Of course." Sandy stood and shook her hand. "I'm here for a couple more days. Call me and we'll rearrange. I hope everything is okay."

Haze smiled her thanks. Landing a big client was the last thing on her mind right then, but she was grateful he would give her another chance. Her only concern was getting to London and bringing Gabby home. Even if Gabby only wanted to be friends, Haze was done missing her. She wanted her home.

"It will be."

†

Haze pulled up outside Gabby's parents' house. She hadn't been there for a few years, but it looked the same. She'd driven straight from her meeting, not giving herself a second to change her mind. She had been thinking to come there for a couple of weeks anyway. Seeing Nikki with Rhea had tipped her over in favour of the journey. She wasn't sure Gabby would even want to see her, but she needed to try.

She hurried up the walkway and rang the bell. A moment later, Gabby's mother opened the door. The resemblance between mother and daughter was striking.

"Hi. I don't know if you remember me. I'm a friend of Gabby's."

Narrowed eyes looked Haze up and down, causing her to blush. "Hazel. Right?"

"Yes." Haze glanced over Claire's shoulder into the foyer, half expecting to see Gabby behind her. "Is she here?"

"She's up in her room, taking a nap."

Haze's stomach clenched. "Is everything okay with the baby?"

"Everything is fine." Claire smiled reassuringly and stepped back, allowing Haze to enter. "She's just tired."

"Do you think she would mind if I talked to her?"

Claire closed the door and folded her arms across her ample breasts, clicking her tongue. "You're very fond of my daughter, aren't you?"

"Yes, I am," Haze replied, sticking her hands in her trouser pockets so Claire wouldn't see them shaking. She was nervous and worried she was about to get the third degree for liking a married woman.

"It's none of my business, and you don't have to tell me, but what do you think of Gabby's situation with Nicole?"

That Nicole is a fool for ever hurting Gabby. "All I want is for Gabby and the baby to be happy and healthy. If that's with Nikki, then I'll be her friend as always." She wanted to blurt out that Nikki was still cheating, but it wasn't her place. That would be Gabby's decision to make if she ever found out. The whole drive up there, Haze had planned to tell Gabby what she had seen. The reality was she didn't want to be the one to cause her any more pain. She knew she was being cowardly and hoped Nikki would have the guts to be honest with Gabby. Besides, she didn't really have any proof Nikki was still with Rhea. *Yeah, right. No one clings to their work colleague the way those two were.*

"And if it's not Nicole she wants?"

"I'll support whatever her decision is. Mrs Carter?" Haze took a breath, giving herself a moment to think. "I assume Gabby told you everything?"

Claire nodded. "She did."

"So then you know I would never do anything to hurt her."

"I do. But remember, forever is a long time. There will be heartache along the way. Just promise to do your best. Gabby can make her own mistakes."

"So you think we would be a mistake?" Haze asked carefully, not sure she really wanted an answer.

"You have all found yourselves in quite a mess. If you are meant to be together, you will be. I will tell you one thing, Hazel." Claire stepped closer. "You've made a very good choice in coming up here. Gabby has been a wreck, and not just over Nicole's behaviour." Her features softened. "She misses you."

Haze's heart gave a start. "I miss her too."

"Then go see her. I'm sure it'll put a smile on her grumpy face."

"Thank you."

Claire turned and walked away, calling over her shoulder. "Second door on the left."

Haze swallowed hard, then climbed the stairs, her heart beating wildly. She had never been so anxious before. She just hoped Gabby would be pleased to see her. She stopped outside the door Claire had indicated and knocked.

†

"Mum, I told you, I'm not hungry." Gabby opened her eyes and glared at the door. Her appetite had fled a few days ago. Everything seemed to make her queasy lately, but her mother wouldn't stop pestering her to eat, telling her the baby needed nourishment. Judging by the size of her stomach, Gabby knew he would be fine. The thought of pushing him out made her cringe. The birthing video her mother made her watch the other night hadn't helped her appetite.

"It's Haze."

Gabby swung her legs off the bed and made two attempts at sitting. Her heartrate tripled, and she wasn't sure if it was the getting up or hearing Haze's voice after so long. She stood and went to the door. "Haze?" She pulled the door open wide. Standing before her was Haze, dressed in a crisp white shirt and tailored trousers. "Oh my God." She lurched forward and grabbed hold of Haze, wrapping her arms around her shoulders. Haze's arms came around her waist, not quite reaching all the way around. "I've missed you so much."

"You've gotten big," Haze mumbled into Gabby's shoulder.

"You know you should never say that to a woman."

Haze pulled back and smiled widely. "Big in a good way." She placed gentle hands on Gabby's bump. "You're blossoming."

"Thank you." Gabby blushed then frowned. "Nicole isn't with you, is she?"

"No. I'm on my own."

Gabby took Haze's hand and pulled her in to sit on the bed with her. She didn't let go. Neither spoke for a moment. Gabby was content to just drink in the sight of Haze sitting before her. It had been a long two months. Although she knew she missed Haze, she hadn't realised just how much until that moment. "What are you doing here?"

"I've come to take you home."

"What?"

Haze looked away for a moment, her forehead creasing. "Gabby, the last two months have been hell. On all of us. The one thing I know for sure is that I've missed you." She reached up and cupped Gabby's cheek. "I have no right to ask, and you can tell me to get lost, but will you move back into my place? At least until you know what you'll do."

"I need to tell you something before I agree to anything."

Haze's hand dropped, chewing her lip. "Okay."

"It's about Nicole."

"You want to go back to her?" Haze frowned. "That's fine. I just don't want to lose your friendship."

"Haze, shut up for a minute and let me talk. You asked me to leave because you said I couldn't make up my mind. What you don't know is that I made my mind up the first morning I saw you sleeping on your couch, I just didn't know it then." She took Haze's hand again and spoke her truth. "I don't want to go back to Nicole. I don't love her anymore." She shook her head. "But I'm not ready to start anything with you either. The baby is due in a month, and I have a lot to sort out. I need some time to get back on my feet." *That's if the swelling ever goes down.* "It wouldn't be fair to Nicole if you and I got together right away." She had no doubt she wanted to be with Haze, but no way she would be doing anything with her when her body was about to be bruised and battered giving birth. *Oh God, what if it doesn't go back to how it looked before?* "I still have a lot to figure out. And I need to tell Nicole it's over for good." One conversation she wasn't looking forward to.

"So what are you saying?"

"If I come back with you, it has to be as friends. Nothing can happen, not yet anyway."

"But you like me?"

"You know I do."

Haze grinned quickly. "But nothing can happen?"

Gabby shook her head. "Not for a while." *Not until my bits look human again.*

"I can live with that. And to be honest, I'm still not sure it'll be a good idea anyway. Nikki was my friend."

"Was your friend?"

Haze waved her off. "It's nothing, don't worry about it."

Something had clearly happened between them in the time Gabby was away, but it was clear Haze didn't want to talk about it. Gabby hoped it wasn't about her, but she wasn't stupid. Haze was loyal to everyone. For her not to be Nicole's friend after all this time, something big must have happened. "So we're in the same position as before. Attracted to each other, but with no chance of anything happening."

"No, this is different."

"How?"

"I no longer feel like you're using me to get back at Nicole."

"You thought that?"

"For a while, yes."

"I'm so sorry." She squeezed her hand, hating Haze had ever felt that way. She couldn't blame her. Gabby only admitted the attraction after she caught Nicole cheating.

"It's okay. A lot has happened. Now we can move on." Haze cleared her throat. "I was thinking, if it's alright with you, maybe we can add a few things to the flat. A cot and changing table, that sort of thing."

"Haze, that's sweet of you to offer, but I can't take over your room, not with a baby too. Your back will soon give out sleeping on the couch."

"I can rearrange my office, make room for a bed. I've picked up some more clients, so I could even rent some office space if need be. It's no problem. I just want you home. It can even be temporary until you find somewhere permanent. Just please come back with me."

Gabby gazed at her for a long moment. Haze looked so earnest and hopeful, she found herself agreeing. She had no intention of going back to her old home anyway. Staying with Haze made sense, while she figured something else out. "Okay, yes."

"Yes?"

"Yes. Nothing would make me happier."

"Thank you." Haze wrapped her in a hug.

"No, thank you for coming here to get me. If you hadn't, I probably would have hidden out here forever."

Gabby rose from the bed and dragged her duffle out from underneath. She began to pack the few things she had brought when she had left Haze's.

"Has Nikki tried calling lately?" Haze asked, as she repacked clothing Gabby was throwing into the bag.

"No. I've tried calling her and messaged her a few times, but she never replied. I assume she's busy." Gabby had called Nicole over a dozen times in the last week alone. So much for her wanting a fresh start. Gabby didn't mind Nicole wasn't making the effort to talk, but she was irked she couldn't even be bothered to return her calls. Especially as she needed to tell her it was over. "Has she spoke to you at all?"

"I've only seen her a couple of times. I couldn't face her, knowing why you left."

"Well, she's probably back in bed with her mistress."

Haze coughed and looked away. "You don't seem upset by that."

"I'm not." Gabby shrugged. "I hate that she cheated on me, but it led me to understand my real feelings for her, and for you. It never would have worked out anyway. I can't trust her, and I don't love her. She can screw anyone she wants now."

"You mean that?"

Gabby stepped up to Haze and took her hands in her own, entwining their fingers. "Yes. We will need to talk. I need to tell her it's over for good and discuss the arrangements for the baby. She is his mother after all. But for anything else between us?" She shook her head. "No, it's done."

"And you're okay with that?" Haze looked up from under her lashes, her hesitation clear.

"I am now you're here." Gabby leaned in and kissed her cheek. "Take me home, Haze."

"You came in your own car. I'll have to follow you."

"You can follow me anywhere."

CHAPTER FOURTEEN

Gabby sat on Haze's sofa, her feet resting on the coffee table. The drive back had been uneventful but exhausting. The only thing keeping her on the road and not pulling off to take a power nap was knowing Haze was only a few cars behind. She still couldn't believe Haze had turned up at her parents' house to convince her to come home. Gabby lost count of how many times she had wished for that very thing. After admitting to her parents it was over with Nicole and that she liked Haze, she had wanted to come back to Bristol. She didn't know how. She couldn't very well just turn up at Haze's again. Had she'd known Haze was missing her terribly and wanted her back, she would have jumped into her car and raced there. Things had worked out well. She was back with Haze, on the cusp of starting a new relationship.

119

Gabby still wasn't sure how to tell Nicole it was over, but as she watched Haze lug her duffle bag through the front door and up the hall, she knew she had made the right decision. Haze was the one she wanted. Why she was waiting until after the baby was born to make a move, she didn't know. Haze didn't seem to care Gabby's growing belly made her look like a whale. *Forget it Gabs, you can't even see your feet. How are you supposed to seduce her when you're bloated everywhere?* No, waiting would be the best thing. Besides, they still had Nicole to deal with.

"How are you feeling?" Haze settled next to Gabby on the couch, her hand innocently lying on Gabby's stomach.

"Tired." She placed her hand on top of Haze's, the warmth of her skin chasing the chill from her own. "It was a long drive, especially with this little guy wriggling all the way home. I don't think he likes it when I'm driving for so long."

"He's probably cramped in there." Haze removed her hand and placed her head there instead. They both laughed when the baby responded with a swift kick.

"I'm not surprised, he feels huge." Gabby sighed, puffing out her cheeks. "I look huge too."

A flash of anger zipped across Haze's features. "You're not huge." She cupped Gabby's cheek. "You're beautiful."

"And you, are a charmer." Gabby smiled at Haze's belief in her words. It seemed to Gabby that Haze really did think she was beautiful, no matter her size. Her heart thrummed in her chest, feeling desired for the first time in months. She hadn't felt that way when she slept with Nicole two months ago. Yes, Nicole said the right things, made the right moves, but there was no connection. Gabby was more turned on now by the look in Haze's eyes then she ever was with Nicole.

How could I have married her when I have such passion for Haze? Some questions would never be answered. There were more pressing needs. "What do you want for supper?"

"How about we order something? I'm too exhausted to cook," Haze admitted.

"Sounds good."

"I'll grab the menus." Haze rose and headed to the kitchen, coming back a moment later and handing the menus to Gabby. "Here you go. I'll have anything you're having." They made their choices, and Haze ordered the delivery using a phone app. She had just put her mobile down when Gabby's began ringing.

"That's mine."

"Stay there, I'll get it." Haze found the phone in Gabby's coat pocket draped over the armchair and handed it over. "Here."

"Thanks." Gabby glanced at the caller ID. "It's Nicole."

"I'll give you some privacy."

"No." Gabby held out her free hand to Haze. "Stay. Please."

Haze frowned, then took her hand, sitting close to her on the couch. "Okay."

Gabby took a breath and answered. "Hello, Nicole."

"Hey, babe. Sorry I missed your calls. My phone has been playing up, so didn't get your messages. How are you?"

Nicole sounded upbeat, too upbeat, like she was forcing herself to put a lighter tone in her inflection. After two months of no contact, you'd think she'd sound a little concerned. "I'm fine."

"You've not been in touch for weeks. I was beginning to worry."

Nicole said the right thing, but the voice was all wrong. Gabby had known her long enough to hear when Nicole really cared about something. This wasn't it. *Did she even care I left?* "I've tried calling you for three weeks now."

"I just explained why I didn't get your calls." Anger slipped into Nicole's voice. "Look, I don't want to argue. When are you coming home?"

"Actually, I am home."

"What?"

"I got back to Haze's about an hour ago." Gabby glanced at Haze, who looked at her with a pensive expression. Nicole didn't reply for several long beats.

"Haze's?"

"Yes." Haze squeezed her hand, obviously able to hear Nicole through the phone.

"Why? I thought we agreed to sell the house and find somewhere new for us."

"Nicole, I need to talk to you about that, but not over the phone."

"What has she told you? Whatever it is, it isn't true." Her voice had risen, but Gabby didn't miss the panic in her tone.

"I have no idea what you're talking about. I came back here because I wanted to. We need to meet up and discuss a few things."

"I don't believe this. We slept together. You said you would forgive me. Now it sounds like you're leaving me for good."

"Nicole, please. Just meet me somewhere so we can talk."

"I'm busy completing the merger for the rest of the week. It'll have to wait." The line went dead.

"Nicole?" Gabby tossed the phone on to the coffee table harder than she intended. "She hung up on me. What the hell is going on with her?"

"Who knows?"

Haze stared straight ahead, avoiding Gabby's questioning gaze. It wasn't lost on Gabby that Haze was hiding something. She was a crap liar. Gabby could always read her. Avoidance of eye contact was proof Haze knew more than she tried to let on. "I think you do. Haze, what happened when I was away?"

"Nothing. I told you, I haven't really seen her much." Haze folded her arms across her chest.

"You're lying. You said in London she wasn't your friend. What happened to make you not want to be her friend anymore?"

"I swear, nothing happened. I just don't like what she did to you." She took a breath, relaxing her arms. She gazed at Gabby, her eyes moistening with the threat of tears. Gabby took her hand. "I tried to forgive her for that, but I can't. It doesn't help I like you more than I should. I can't see her, knowing how much she hurt you. I want to kill her for doing that to you."

"I'm tired of this whole situation. I don't like that I've come between you two."

"You didn't do anything. Nikki did. She is the one who has ruined everything."

Gabby didn't totally agree with that statement. Nicole may have cheated, but weren't Haze and Gabby the ones sitting there holding hands, sharing their mutual attraction? Nicole may have started the whole thing, but it was Gabby and Haze that were close to crossing a line that would irrevocably break the trio up. It would be easy for Gabby to walk away from Nicole and never see her again. If not for the baby, she would be fine with that. But Haze and Nicole had been friends for ever. If Gabby and Haze got together, Nicole would never speak to either of them again. *Maybe being with Haze is a bad idea.*

"We still have each other, right?" Gabby needed to gauge Haze's feelings on it all.

"Yes. You, me, and Junior."

"Junior?" Haze shrugged, her cheeks tinting an adorable shade of pink. A slither of doubt set up residence in Gabby's stomach. They were attracted to each other, but what about the baby? Did Haze even want to be a parent? "How do you feel about me being pregnant?"

Haze squinted at her, her forehead creasing. "What? I think it's great. I can't wait to see you being a mother." She grinned, placing their joined hands on the bump. "It's going to be awesome."

"What about you?"

"What about me?"

"Haze, if anything were to happen between us, there'd be a kid involved. We come as a package deal. You've never mentioned wanting kids before. How do you feel about that?"

"You're right. Kids weren't something I ever saw myself having." Haze grinned, her gaze full of love. "But your baby? I would be honoured to be involved with him any way you want me to be. Nikki will be his mum, but I wouldn't mind being a step-mum." Her voice dropped to a murmur, the huskiness causing Gabby's lower stomach to clench. "I could teach him to draw. Show him how PCs work. Even give him hints when it comes to picking up the ladies when he's older."

Gabby laughed. "You are quite good in that department. When you're not running away."

"Yeah. You have no idea how many times I regretted legging it after we kissed." Haze scooted closer so their thighs touched, and placed her arm along the back of the sofa behind Gabby's head. "Watching you date Nikki, then get married, I couldn't help but wonder what it would have been like if you were with me." She tilted her head closer to Gabby's. "I spent years being jealous of her. Being able to touch you. Kiss you. Make love to you."

"Haze." Gabby's breathing increased. Her pulse pounded in her ears. She was certain Haze was going to kiss her.

"It just about killed me, Gabby. All the times we would have a movie night, and you were cuddled up with Nikki on the sofa. I'd sit there with a giant knot of tension in my gut, wishing it was me. Then you'd go to bed together."

Gabby didn't miss the pain in her gaze. She wished she had known. *And what would you have done? You were with Nicole.*

"I'd lay there, wide awake, listening to you both laugh and giggle. Many a night, I would cry myself to sleep because I couldn't have you."

"I had no idea." Gabby reached up and swept Haze's hair away from her face, then rested her palm against her cheek. "I'm sorry."

Haze shook her head slightly. "It's not your fault. It was my problem." She smiled. "And then one night you turned up at my door. Your world had fallen apart. Nikki had cheated."

"And I finally admitted I was attracted to you."

"Which started off another set of emotions and heartache. I missed you so very much these past months."

125

"I missed you too."

Haze's gaze dropped to Gabby's lips and back up to her eyes. "Are you sure it's over with Nikki?"

"So very sure. Hazel—" The knock at the door caused them both to spring apart, both breathing rapidly.

"Shit. That'll be the food."

"Perfect timing."

Haze paid the delivery driver, then carried the food into the kitchen. Gabby was glad of the reprieve. She had no doubt if they hadn't been interrupted, she would have begged Haze to take her to bed. It was too soon. She had only recently decided to end things with Nicole, and it wouldn't be fair to either of them if Gabby slept with Haze before talking to her. Not only that, Gabby felt bloated and so unsexy. Judging by the look in Haze's eyes a moment ago, Haze didn't care.

Haze came back in the lounge carrying two plates of steaming curry. By unspoken agreement, they ate in silence.

Fifteen minutes later, Gabby said, "That was delicious." Haze took her plate. "Best curry I've had in a long time."

"You do know that spicy food can start labour?" Haze said once she had returned the plates to the kitchen and sat in the armchair. Gabby didn't comment on the distance Haze had put between them. It was probably for the best.

"That's a myth."

"You'd better hope so. He's not ready to come out yet. About earlier—"

"Haze, it's fine." Gabby waved her hand dismissively. "Things got a little out of hand."

"But you wanted to kiss me?" Haze flushed, her gaze focused on the far wall.

"More than anything."

Haze swallowed hard then stood, stuffing her hands in her pockets. "You'd better get to bed, before we do anything we might regret."

Regret? No, I won't ever regret doing anything with you. "Yes, you're right." Now wasn't the time. Haze helped her off the couch, but Gabby couldn't go to bed without at least one kiss. She leaned up on her tiptoes and quickly pecked Haze's lips. The lingering taste of curry mixed with Haze's unique flavour. It wasn't nearly enough contact, but Gabby stepped away. *Now isn't the time.* "Goodnight, Haze."

"Goodnight, Gabby. Thank you for coming home."

"Thank you for coming to get me."

Haze grinned widely. "No problem."

Gabby readied for bed and settled under the covers, a huge smile on her face. Despite the odd conversation with Nicole on the phone, the very long day had ended pleasantly. For the first time since Gabby walked in on Nicole with another woman, she was finally looking forward to the future. A future with Haze.

†

Late the next afternoon, Haze sat at the kitchen table, a cold bottle of beer in front of her. She'd had a busy day. The rescheduled meeting at the hotel with Sandy had gone well. She told him to think about things before deciding, but he didn't need to. He even handed over a hefty deposit, so she could get started designing his website. Knowing her bank balance was padded a little more, she left the hotel and headed straight to the shopping centre to buy the things she had promised for the baby.

127

Her spending got a little out of hand. It took four trips to the car and back to get it all inside the flat. Three hours later, her bedroom was all kitted out for Junior's arrival. She even managed to change up her office, so she had room to sleep in there instead of on the couch in the living room. She couldn't wait for Gabby to get home from seeing Edith, excited to show her everything she had done.

A smile formed on her lips, as she swirled the bottle on the table. Having Gabby home was the best feeling ever. Gabby may not be ready to start a romantic relationship with her, but Haze knew they were heading in that direction. She still debated whether to tell Gabby she had seen Nikki in the hotel lobby with Rhea. It would only upset Gabby. Gabby said it was over between them anyway, so there really was no point in hurting her if she didn't need to.

She took a sip of her beer and heard the front door open. A moment later, Gabby strolled into the kitchen, plonking herself down on a chair and letting out a heavy sigh. She looked tired. The baby was due in less than three weeks, and it was clear from her exhaustion she couldn't wait to get him out.

"Hey." Gabby's smile didn't quite reach her eyes. "How did your meeting go?"

"It was good. He signed the contract and left a deposit. I gave him a list of things I need for the website, then I can start putting it together."

"That's great." Gabby beamed and reached across the table, taking one of Haze's hands. "I'm so happy for you."

"Thanks. He's a big client. If I do a good job, I'm hoping it'll lead to more business."

"I'm sure you'll smash it."

"How's Edith?"

"She's great. Says she misses me around the school. She hasn't got anyone to moan to, so she's taken up boxing."

"Wow. At her age?"

"Yeah. I guess you're never too old to try something new." Gabby reached up behind her head trying to rub her back. Haze stood and moved Gabby's arm out of the way, massaging the tight muscles. Gabby let out a groan, dipping her head forward so Haze could get better access to her neck.

"Is she still okay with you being off work?"

"She says she is, but I could tell she can't wait to have me back. It's nice to fit in somewhere." There was a wistful tone to Gabby's voice.

"You miss it, don't you?"

"Yes. I never would have thought I'd miss grumpy teenagers, but I do."

"When do you think you'll go back?"

"I'm not sure. I'm going to be a single mum, and I still don't have anywhere to live."

Haze stopped her massage, bending down to kiss Gabby's neck, then sat to her left. "I told you, you can stay here as long as you like."

Gabby smiled. "I know, and thank you, but living here permanently isn't an option. This is your home and office. You aren't going to want a crying baby around all day when you're trying to work."

"I'll invest in some earplugs." Haze grinned, then turned serious. She wanted Gabby to know just how much she wanted her there. "I promise, Gabby, it's not a problem."

"Tell me that again when he's screaming for his middle of the night feed."

Knowing Gabby wouldn't believe her words, she decided it was the perfect time to show Gabby her surprise. She rose from the chair and held out her hand, helping Gabby stand. "I have something to show you. Come with me."

Haze led them down the hall and into the bedroom. She stood back, so Gabby could take in all the details. Haze had moved the bed over to the far side, making room for the oak cot and matching changing table. A three-foot bookcase held nappies and wet wipes, baby-grows, and blankets. She had also purchased bottles, steriliser, and dummies, as well as a few toys that Haze knew he wouldn't need for months.

"Oh my God. Haze, it's incredible." Gabby stood by the cot, running her hand over the fleece blanket. She turned on the mobile that hung over the top and glanced at Haze with tears in her eyes.

"I went a little overboard. I wasn't sure what you already had at the house, so I figured I'd just get everything." Haze couldn't stop the blush that warmed her skin. She stuffed her hands in her pockets.

"You must have spent a fortune." Gabby frowned. "I can't let you do this, it's too expensive. Tell me how much, and I'll transfer it over to you."

Haze shook her head. "No."

"Haze." Gabby glared at her, but Haze wouldn't be swayed.

"No. It's my gift to you and Junior." She stepped toward Gabby, taking one of her hands in her own. "Gabby, you have a lot going on right now. Please, let me do this for you."

Gabby reached up and ran the back of her fingers down Haze's cheek. "You're so sweet. Thank you." She glanced back at the cot, reaching in to pull out a small, blue teddy bear that glowed when you pressed his belly. "You even got him a cuddly night light."

"He looked so cute, I had to get him."

"Thank you." Gabby leaned up and kissed Haze's cheek. "But what about you? You can't keep sleeping on the couch."

"Ah, that's the other thing." Haze smiled widely. She took Gabby's hand again. "Come on." She opened her office door wide and pulled Gabby into the room. "I got a sofa bed, so I can put it up if I need more space." She was lucky the guy selling it had been able to deliver it for her. Of course, it cost her extra, but it was worth it. "With the monitors now on the wall, I didn't need such a large desk, so I had room for the chest of drawers."

"What about your easel?"

Haze went to the far wall and unclipped a fold-up desk that served the purpose of an easel. "Voila! I don't do much drawing these days anyway, but I can pull it down when I need it." She did enjoy drawing freehand, but computer graphics were her real passion. Not having the easel up all the time saved space. With all the changes she had made to the office, she could comfortably sleep and work all in the same room. Haze had even bought a room divider from a charity shop to separate the bed from the office side of things.

"You've thought of everything, haven't you?"

Haze shrugged. "I told you, I want you to stay. Even if nothing happens between us, I want you to live here for as long as you need to. There is no rush for you to go. Once Junior gets here, you can take as much time as you need to get back into a routine before you think about leaving."

"Are you sure this won't intrude on your life too much?"

"Gabby, I work and sleep. That's about it. Your being here isn't an imposition."

"Thank you. I don't know what I would have done without you."

"You never have to find out."

Haze was pleased with herself. Gabby seemed happy about all the changes she had made, and Haze hoped this would mean she wouldn't think about leaving anytime soon. It was too early to be living together in a romantic sense. They had separate rooms and would basically be housemates. If things went the way Haze hoped, it would be easy enough to change her office into a nursery and share the bedroom with Gabby. Renting office space wouldn't be a problem either, especially if she acquired more high-end clients. For the first time in a long while, Haze thought things were finally coming together for her.

CHAPTER FIFTEEN

Sitting close together on the sofa, having one of their many movie nights without Nikki there was fine with Haze. She had dreamed of this very thing, but it had always been Gabby and Nikki together. Sitting there with Gabby's head resting on her shoulder, able to wrap an arm around her back, was something Haze had always wished for. The curtains were drawn, the lights dimmed, and the heating was on. A fleece blanket covered their lower halves, and it was the most cosiest and relaxed Haze had ever been.

"I can't believe I'm crying." Gabby reached up to wipe her eyes.

Haze chuckled and kissed her temple. "Gabby, it's just a film. An animation at that." They were watching Toy Story

3, and yeah, Haze found some of it a little emotional. She wasn't openly crying like Gabby. It was cute.

"I can't help it. My hormones are driving me crazy."

"I'd suggest watching another, but I don't think there are enough tissues left in the house." Gabby rewarded her with a thump on the thigh.

"Very funny." Gabby flung off the blanket and shuffled forward, trying but failing to rise from the couch. She flopped back with a groan. "Ugh. I can't wait for him to come out. I've never been so ungraceful in my life."

"What about when we all went ice skating and you flailed around for ages before you dumped yourself on your ass?" That had been one of the funniest sights Haze had ever seen. Gabby had lost her balance and it seemed to Haze her legs and arms were freewheeling forever before finally losing to gravity and hitting the ice, hard.

"That was mortifying." Gabby covered her face with her hands. "All those kids laughed at me."

"It was pretty funny."

Gabby thumped her again, then started to tickle her sides, the thing Haze hated most in the world, although she couldn't stop laughing.

"Whoa, stop it." Haze managed to get away from Gabby, jumping off the sofa with a triumphant grin on her face as Gabby tried to follow suit. Haze laughed when Gabby collapsed back against the cushions. She wasn't quite out of reach. Gabby lunged forward and grabbed her arm, pulling her down to the couch. "Oomph."

"You should never tease a pregnant lady."

"Why? What are you going to do about it?" Haze waggled her eyebrows. Gabby's playful side had been missing for a long time, and Haze was glad she was able to perk her up.

"Shut you up," came Gabby's menacing reply.

"Oh yeah? How?"

"Like this."

Gabby caught the back of Haze's head and brought her closer. Haze didn't have time to react as Gabby's mouth was on hers. The memory of their first kiss paled in comparison to this. Gabby's lips were silky soft, her tongue strong and demanding. Haze reached out and cupped her face, holding her firmly in place. One of Gabby's hands wound its way under Haze's T-shirt and settled on her ribs, close to her breast. All the breath left in Haze whooshed out, as Gabby's hand tensed on her skin. Although the room was hot, Haze couldn't suppress the shiver that coursed through her body. Gabby reclaimed her mouth, her hand going higher and grazing the cotton of her sports bra. Somehow, Haze had managed to shift them both, so she was straddling Gabby's thigh. The only thing that prevented Haze lying completely on her was the bump protruding from Gabby's belly. Haze was losing control. She could already feel how wet her underwear was, her clit twitching for release.

"Gabby, we should stop."

"Why?"

"For one thing, you're eight and a half months pregnant. Two, I'm about to embarrass myself just from kissing you."

Gabby grinned and kissed her again. "Yeah?"

"Hmm hmm."

"How about if I do this?" Gabby ran her hand over Haze's denim covered ass and lifted her own thigh to crush against Haze's centre. The pressure nearly tipped Haze over the edge.

"Gabby, please." Haze used all the will power she had left to climb off Gabby and stand as far away as she could. "I can't control myself around you."

"That's a good thing, though, right?" Gabby's skin was flushed, her gaze roaming over Haze with liquid passion.

"Oh, it's a very good thing."

"You realise, once Junior gets here, it'll be a while before I'm in any condition to do anything?"

"Being with you is more than just sex." Haze knelt next to the sofa, helping Gabby into a sitting position. Haze cupped her cheek, running her thumb over swollen lips. "I'd be happy just to sleep next to you for the rest of our lives."

"That's sweet, but I'm not." Gabby grinned wickedly and bit the tip of Haze's thumb playfully. "I want your naked body on mine."

"Gabby. You're not making this easy."

"Sorry."

"Liar." The ringing of a mobile interrupted them.

"That's my phone," Gabby said. Haze stood and retrieved it from the kitchen. She handed it to Gabby and sat on the arm of the couch, her hand going to Gabby's shoulder. "Hello? Oh, hey…Yeah, okay…that's fine…I'll see you then." Gabby disconnected and tossed the phone onto the cushion next to her. "That was Nicole. She wants to take me out to dinner tomorrow night to discuss our future."

"Why does she need to take you to dinner for that?" Haze tried to not let the jealousy flair up, but it was hard. Gabby and Nikki had a lot of history. As much as Gabby said it was over between them, she still hadn't told Nikki that. Nikki was a charmer; it wouldn't surprise Haze if her charms worked on Gabby.

"I don't know. Perhaps she thinks if we're in a restaurant I won't make a scene."

"She might be trying to woo you."

Gabby turned with a questioning gaze. "Woo me?"

"You know what I mean." Haze shrugged and waved her hand in the air. "Make a good impression."

"Well, it won't work." Gabby gave Haze's thigh a reassuring squeeze. "I told you, Haze, I want to be with you. What we were doing a minute ago should be proof of that."

"I know, but I can't help feeling it's all going to go wrong."

"Everything will be fine. I'll go to dinner, tell her it's over, and we can all move on."

"Will you tell her about us?" Haze couldn't look at Gabby.

"No, not yet. I don't think that's fair."

"You're right. I don't fancy getting my ass kicked."

Gabby grinned. "I think you could take her."

"You think so?"

"Yeah." She looked Haze up and down, her grin widening. "You're all lean muscle and strength."

"I'm just a big softie."

"I know. And I lov...like that about you." Gabby slapped her own thighs and attempted to push off the sofa. Haze laughed, then helped her to stand. "I'm going to go for my hundredth pee of the day. You pick a movie." She walked toward the hall and called over her shoulder. "Make it a happy one. With all the peeing and crying, I'm severely dehydrated."

Haze laughed loudly and went to the cabinet under the TV. She scanned the DVDs, then smiled as her eye caught Finding Dory. She pulled the case from the rack, knowing it would bring Gabby to tears again. It was a mean thing to do, to make her cry, but if it meant Gabby would snuggle under a blanket with her while she wept, Haze was all for it.

CHAPTER SIXTEEN

The knock on the door startled Haze, even though she was expecting it. Nikki was coming to take Gabby out for dinner to talk about their future. She couldn't shake the ball of tension that had sprung up in her gut since Nikki phoned the day before. The rest of their evening had been great. Gabby cried over Dory, as Haze knew she would. They shared a quiet meal, before retiring to their own rooms for the night. Gabby had said she wasn't looking forward to going out with Nikki but knew she had to, so she could tell her it was over. Haze's fear of Nikki winning Gabby back wouldn't go away.

She stood from the couch and opened the door. Nikki looked stunning, dressed in a light blue evening gown that showed off her tanned legs. Her makeup was expertly applied and lent an air of sophistication to her presence. Haze glanced down at her own jogging bottoms and ratty T-shirt. The differences between them were apparent. Haze never fitted into the glamour mold. Not for the first time, she thought Gabby was too good for her. *Why have a mess like me when you can have that?*

"Nikki."

"Hello, Haze." Nikki stepped through the doorway, her perfume tickling Haze's nose. "Is Gabby ready?"

"She'll be out in a minute." Haze closed the door and followed Nikki into the lounge.

"How are you?"

"I'm fine. You?" Nikki's smile was radiant. Haze wanted to slap it off her face.

"I'm great. Thank you for convincing her to come home. Maybe now we can move on from all this mess and get back to normal."

"What about Rhea?"

Anger flashed across Nikki's features, making her appear dangerous. "That's over with." She reached into her handbag and pulled out a small velvet box. She checked the hallway for movement. "Look, I bought this for Gabby." She opened the lid, and a huge diamond ring glistened back at Haze.

"Looks expensive."

"Hell yeah. Over three grand." Nikki snapped the box shut and stuffed it back in her bag. "I'm going to re-propose tonight. Show her I'm serious about us getting back together."

"Do you really think a sparkly diamond will make her forget what you did?" *How could you possibly believe she'd want that? And surely you'd want all the money you could get for the baby?*

"This is none of your business. By tomorrow night, Gabby will be back home with me, and we'll be starting a family together. If you still want to be friends with us, you'd better accept it and move on yourself. I won't have you coming between us." Nikki's demeanour shifted. Her face relaxed, and Haze realised Gabby must have come into the room. "Hello, sweetheart. It's been so long."

Haze watched, as Nikki approached Gabby with a huge smile on her face. Nikki kissed her cheek, taking her hands in her own. Haze's stomach flipped. "You look fabulous."

"Hello, Nicole." Gabby's gaze found Haze's, and she smiled slightly.

"Are you ready to go? I booked your favourite restaurant."

"What?" Gabby looked back at Nicole. "Oh, yes. Um, if you go wait in the car, I just need to visit the little girls' room."

"Sure thing." Nicole kissed her cheek again. "I'll be waiting." The front door closed behind her.

"Haze—"

"You look really nice, Gabby." Despite being nearly nine months pregnant, Gabby looked radiant. Haze knew she had maternity trousers on, but the flowing blouse that hung in waves around her waist and over her bump made her outfit look elegant. A thin silver chain circled her neck, and a matching watch adorned her wrist.

Low heels added height to Gabby, matching Haze's own. She could see directly into Gabby's eyes. She didn't know why Gabby had made such an effort if all she was going to do was dump Nikki. To Haze, it looked like she was dressing for a date. She hoped that wasn't how Gabby felt.

141

"Thank you. Haze, you know nothing will happen between Nicole and me, don't you?"

Haze shrugged a shoulder. "Of course."

"You don't seem so sure." Gabby frowned, her brows pinching above the bridge of her nose.

"It's just…God, I don't know, Gabby. Maybe you would be better off with her. She can afford to take care of you." She thought of the ring in Nikki's handbag. Haze would never be able to afford something like that, not without saving for years. Her modest home and small business were enough for her but would never match up to what Nikki earned.

"Financially, yes." Gabby tapped her chest. "But she can't take care of my heart. Not the way I need her to, and certainly not the way you do." She stepped closer, taking one of Haze's hands. "Please, Haze, don't worry. I'm going to tell her it's over. I'm coming home to you." Gabby leaned in and kissed her softly on the lips.

"You really do look nice."

Gabby blushed. "Thank you. I'll see you soon."

"Okay."

Haze helped Gabby into her long wool overcoat and opened the door. Watching Nikki kiss her cheek again and open the car door for her was one of the hardest things Haze had witnessed. She wanted to call out to her, beg her not to go, tell her that Nikki was still a cheat. Her lips remained tightly clamped together. She prayed Gabby would be coming home to her as she promised.

She closed the door and headed to her room. Maybe if I get some work done it'll take my mind off Nikki proposing again. What if Gabby says yes? She didn't really think she would, but a kernel of fear made itself known.

✝

Gabby stared out the window of the moving car, listening as Nicole chatted away as if they hadn't been separated for months. Gabby nodded in the right places, adding the occasional question, but she wasn't interested in small talk. This was a bad idea. She should have declined the dinner and just gone to the house to tell her it was over. From the dress Nicole was wearing, she clearly thought this was a date. Haze thought the same thing. Gabby recalled the look on her face when Nicole had kissed her cheek. It wasn't hard to miss the sadness and confusion in her eyes. Haze had been through so much since Gabby turned up at her door four months ago, not knowing where she stood. *And I've made it worse by going on a date with Nicole. She must hate me.* All Gabby wanted to do was go home and curl up with Haze on the couch like they had last night. It had been a perfect evening, the teasing and crying. The kisses they shared were the highlight and felt as good as the first time. The desire she felt for Haze was so much stronger than she ever had for Nicole. She did love Nicole, had been attracted to her. She wouldn't have married her otherwise. But the heat she had with Haze was beyond compare. *And now I'm here and she's at home, wondering if I'm going to go back to Nicole.*

Nicole pulled the car to a stop. She got out and came around Gabby's side to help her from the seat. The Bistro in the heart of Bristol's town centre was a tearoom by day and a trendy restaurant by night. Gabby and Nicole had found the restaurant by accident, and they'd been regular visitors ever since. The food was always delicious and the staff pleasant. Gabby's stomach flipped at the thought of sharing a meal with Nicole. She needed to tell her it was over, and soon. Being away from Haze was tearing her apart. She wanted to get back and tell her everything was alright.

"This really is a great place," Nicole said as they were shown to the table. The maître d' pulled out the chairs for both of them.

"Yes. It's always been one of my favourites."

"Did I mention how nice you look?"

"Once or twice."

Nicole smiled and reached across the table to take her hand, but Gabby quickly hid them under the table. Nicole's smile turned into a frown. She drew her hand back and smoothed her hair. "Well, you do. Even with your stomach so big."

"Excuse me?" Surely she didn't just say that. "I'm carrying our child."

"I know." Nicole took a sip of water. "What's the matter?"

"Nothing." Thankfully, a waiter approached the table, saving Gabby from her anger.

"Good evening, ladies. Are you ready to order?"

"Can we have a few minutes?" Nicole asked.

"Of course. Just give me a wave when you're ready."

Once he walked away, Gabby spoke first, wanting to tell Nicole it was over before Nicole carried on insulting her and acting like this was a date. "Nicole, we need to talk—"

"So the merger is complete now. Two hundred more employees to oversee and a larger office for me." Nicole beamed across the table. It was obvious how proud she was of the new deal.

"Congratulations. I know how hard you worked for that."

"Thanks. Of course, it means longer hours, but it's worth it. You won't have to go back to that school again."

Gabby narrowed her eyes. "Why not?"

"You won't need to. With my pay rise, there really is no need for you to work. You can raise the baby, and I'll earn the money."

Gabby blinked, her mouth open in shock. *Does she really think I'd be her trophy wife, raising the kids and playing housekeeper?* Sure, Nicole's job was hard. She worked long days and earned way more money than Gabby, but Gabby had her own dreams, her own goals she wanted to achieve. Even if they were together, Gabby would never do that.

"There are so many things wrong with that statement," Gabby said through gritted teeth.

"Huh?"

How did I ever marry her? Surely she wasn't always like this? "I will be going back to teaching as soon as I'm able. That's my career. I have never once agreed to be a stay-at-home mum."

"But—"

"No. End of discussion. Not that it'll concern—"

"I've found a little countryside bungalow for us. It's adorable. The estate agent gave me a tour the other day. You'll love it." Nicole opened her menu, oblivious to Gabby glaring at her with arms folded across her chest.

"Nicole," Gabby ground out.

"I forgive you, by the way, for going back home for two months and not keeping in contact." Nicole glanced up, then back to the menu. "I understand you needed time to think."

"You forgive me?"

"Yeah. You know, we slept together and then you left. I felt pretty crappy after that."

"I'm sorry?"

"It's fine, I said I forgive you."

"I wasn't apologising."

"Oh." Nicole frowned. "Well, it's fine. You're home now, and we can start looking to the future."

Gabby drew in a deep breath. This was getting out of hand. Nicole was waffling on as if nothing had happened between them, like Gabby hadn't caught her cheating. She was planning a future without Gabby's input. This had to stop. It was time to end this.

"Nicole, there is no future. Not for us."

Nicole looked up, the fine lines around her eyes deepening when she squinted at Gabby. "What do you mean?"

"I don't want to be with you anymore."

"I don't understand."

"I'm no longer in love with you. It's over."

"Why would you say that? You agreed to come here with me."

"Yes. To talk to you."

Nicole glanced around, then lowered her voice. "You're dumping me in a restaurant?"

"I didn't want to tell you like this, but you were rambling on. I had to say something."

Nicole sat back and folded her arms across her chest, pursing her lips for a moment. "Is this because Haze saw me at the hotel last week? I told her nothing was going on. Rhea and I were meeting a client."

"Rhea?" Gabby always had the nagging doubt Nicole hadn't stopped seeing her. This was confirmation. *Thank God I didn't take her back. She would have cheated on me forever.*

"Yes. She's back on the project. Haze saw me and assumed the worst. I can only imagine the things she told you."

"She never told me she saw you." *Haze lied to me?* The one thing Gabby could rely on was Haze's honesty. Now it seemed she was lying to her too.

"She didn't?"

"No."

"Oh."

"You were in a hotel with Rhea?"

"Yes, for a business meeting."

"Right." Gabby couldn't resist the eye roll. How many business meetings had Nicole had while screwing Rhea over the months? Gabby didn't dare to guess.

"I swear, Gabby. There's only you."

"I don't believe you."

"I've got you this." She reached into her handbag that was hanging over the arm of the chair. She opened the lid, before thrusting a velvet box in front of Gabby. "Look. Isn't it magnificent?"

"What's that for?

"I wanted to wait for the right time, but I guess now will do." Nicole managed to snag one of Gabby's hands, gripping it tightly. "Gabby, I love you. Will you marry me, again?"

Gabby pulled her hand away, nearly knocking over her water. "Nicole, didn't you hear what I said? I don't want to be with you anymore. It's over." She took a breath. "I want a divorce."

"You're not serious."

"I am."

Nicole shut the lid with a loud snap, her fist tightening around the box. "This is all to do with Haze, isn't it? You're sleeping together."

Gabby shook her head and sighed. "No, we're not. What is going on between you and I has nothing to do with Haze. If I'm honest, it was over the minute I walked in on you with Rhea."

"Then why sleep with me again?"

Good question. She couldn't very well tell her it was because she was jealous Haze was on a date with another woman. That would certainly not go down well. "I was confused. Being away made me realise I didn't love you any longer. I'm sorry, but we're done."

"You can't just walk away from us."

"You left first. You didn't give me much choice."

Nicole's angry gaze dropped to the top of Gabby's bump, just visible above the table. "What about the baby?"

"You're his mother. I won't stop you having a relationship with him, but we're not going to be together again."

"I could take him."

"What?" Gabby had felt anger before, but nothing quite like this. A red-hot rage stole through her body, threatening to explode.

"He came from my egg. He belongs to me."

"I carried him for nine months." Her hands tightened into fists where they rested on the table. "He doesn't belong to just you."

"The courts will see it differently."

"You're threatening me?"

"No." Nicole turned her head. For a moment she looked ashamed and sad. It was the most honest Gabby had seen her look in months. "I just meant—"

"Take me home." Gabby stood from the table. She needed to get out of there.

"Let's talk about this."

"No. Either take me now or I'll get a taxi."

"Fine."

They were both silent on the thirty-minute drive back to Haze's. Gabby's heart rate hadn't settled since they left the restaurant, her fear over Nicole taking the baby making her feel sick. She didn't really think Nicole would be that cruel, but after recent events, she didn't really know Nicole at all.

Nicole pulled up outside Haze's, and Gabby opened the door before the vehicle had fully stopped. Nicole grabbed her forearm. "Think about it, Gabby. We belong together."

"No, we don't." Gabby shucked off her hand and struggled from the seat without help. She ducked her head back in. "Not anymore."

CHAPTER SEVENTEEN

Gabby slammed through the front door. Her body shook uncontrollably from the thought Nicole might try to take her baby. Haze jumped up from the couch, her eyes wide.

"Gabby? That was quick."

Raw from the encounter with Nicole, Gabby unleashed her anger at Haze. "Why didn't you tell me you had seen Nicole with Rhea?"

Haze looked to the floor, her shoulders slumping. "I didn't want to upset you."

"When was it?"

"The day I came and got you."

Gabby walked farther into the room, hands on hips. "That was two weeks ago." Haze had all that time to mention it and never did. That hurt most of all. Gabby didn't care Nicole was still sleeping with Rhea, but she did care that Haze could so easily keep something from her. "And you didn't think I had the right to know?"

"I wanted to tell you, but then we got talking and you said it was over with her." Haze moved closer, a panicked look on her face. "I didn't see the point of telling you, when it would have only hurt you."

Gabby stared at her, noting the wide eyes and pulse pounding in her neck. "That was my decision to make." She glanced away, then put voice to the hurt she was feeling inside. "You lied to me."

"No, not really. Gabby, it didn't matter. And I didn't really see anything. They were just in the lobby together." Haze lifted her arms and let them drop. "For all I knew she was telling the truth."

"You don't seriously believe that, do you?" Gabby sat in the armchair.

"No. In my opinion, she's been carrying on with her since you found out."

"That's why you didn't want to be her friend anymore, isn't it?"

"Yes." Haze knelt and took her hand. "I'm sorry."

Gabby gazed at Haze for a moment, seeing her desperation to be forgiven. Gabby knew in her heart Haze would never do anything to hurt her. What Haze said made sense. It didn't matter who Nicole was seeing. By not telling Gabby, Haze had protected her from the anger that surely would have come out. There was no point dwelling on it. Nicole's love life was of no concern to Gabby any longer. Only one thing about Nicole did matter. "She threatened to take Junior."

"What?"

"I told her it was over, and then she proposed. When I said no, she said she could take him as he's from her egg."

Haze's eyes narrowed to slits. "I'm going to kill her."

"You don't think the courts would give her sole custody, do you?"

Haze moved to sit in the chair and shift Gabby onto her lap. She almost felt safe, wrapped tightly in Haze's arms. "I don't know," Haze said. "We can contact a solicitor and get some advice."

Tears filled Gabby's eyes. "I don't know what I would do if she took him away from me."

"I won't let that happen. I promise." Haze leaned in and kissed her quickly on the lips. "I'm sorry I didn't tell you I saw them."

"It's okay."

"No, it's not. I don't want to have any secrets from you. I never want to hurt you."

Gabby cupped her cheek. "You haven't, you couldn't." Her phone vibrated in the pocket of the coat she still wore. She fished it out and glanced at the screen. "It's a message from Nicole."

"What does it say?"

Gabby swiped it open and read. The tight fist that had gripped her heart the moment Nicole threatened her lessened its hold. "She says she sorry things got out of hand. She didn't mean what she said and doesn't want to take him from me. She wants to talk about things again tomorrow."

"I don't trust her."

"Me neither." She put her phone back in her pocket then stood to hang her coat up by the front door. "I can't stop her from seeing him."

"You'll need to sort out an arrangement. Maybe through the courts."

"I need to start divorce proceedings anyway. I'm not sure if they would do the custody thing at the same time."

"We'll talk to a solicitor first thing in the morning."

"Okay."

Haze stood and pulled Gabby into her warm body once again. Gabby rested her head on her shoulder.

"If we do that in the morning, maybe I can see her in the afternoon."

"Shall I come with you?"

"I'm not sure that's a good idea."

"I don't want her to upset you."

Gabby tilted her head back to better see Haze's eyes. "Haze, I'll be fine. She's never physically hurt me."

"Maybe not, but you're due soon." She placed her hand on the bump. "You don't need that kind of stress."

"I'll be okay." As Gabby said the words, a strong cramp gripped her low in the abdomen. It was a pain she had never felt before. "Ow." The cramp came again, and she knew what was happening. Being two weeks early didn't seem to bother Junior.

"Gabby, are you alright?" Haze asked, her voice coloured with worry.

"Ow. No. Shit." Gabby glanced up from her where she leaned on the arm of the couch and smiled through the contraction. "I think Junior's on his way."

Haze's face blanched, her eyes as big as plates. "Oh God. We need to get to the hospital. Stay there, I'll get your bag." Haze rushed off toward the bedroom, swearing after she ran into the door frame. Gabby laughed at her obvious panic. Haze ran back into the lounge, tossing cushions and magazines out of the way. "Keys, keys. Where are my keys?"

"Haze, calm down." Gabby reached out to still her frantic movements. The next few hours were going to be hard enough on Gabby. She needed Haze to be strong and calm to help get her through labour and delivery. "This could take hours yet. There's no rush."

"Right, you're right." Haze ran her hands through her hair a few times, breathing deeply. After a few seconds, Haze smiled and took Gabby's hand.

"That's better." Haze found her keys and then led them out the door. One hand held Gabby's, the other her bag. *This is it. In a few hours, I'm going to be a mum.* "We need to call Nicole," Gabby said after Haze settled her in the car. "She should be there, if she wants to be." Despite the showdown not an hour ago, Gabby would never take the opportunity away from Nicole to witness the birth of their son.

"I'll do it once we get to the hospital."

"Okay." As another contraction hit, Gabby concentrated on her breathing. The first thing she would be asking for was pain relief.

†

"Come on, Gabby. You're doing fine," Haze said as another contraction hit. Gabby had been in labour for five hours, and progressed steadily in the last sixty minutes. The contractions were only minutes apart, soon Junior would be there. True to her word, Haze had texted Nikki as soon as Gabby was booked in on the maternity ward. She hadn't received a reply. Haze didn't know if she should be pleased with that or not. On the one hand, it was only right Nikki got to see the birth. On the other, Haze wanted to be the one to support Gabby.

"This is harder than I expected."

"It'll be over soon." Gabby's face and neck were covered in sweat, her cheeks red with the exhaustion. Her hand gripped Haze's, while Haze's other hand was rubbing her back.

"You'll need to start pushing on the next contraction," the young midwife said. Gabby's legs were open, knees bent. The midwife between them ready to guide Junior out.

"I don't think I can."

"You can do this, Gabby. I know you can." She turned Gabby's head to hold her gaze.

"Where's Nicole? She should be here."

Haze tried not to flinch. "I've texted and called her. She hasn't responded."

"Okay, Gabby, push."

The grip on Haze's hand tightened, as Gabby bared down, pushing with all her might. This repeated over and again for several minutes. Finally, the midwife declared, "I can see the head. A couple more pushes and baby will be out." Gabby screamed, as she tried again.

The door burst open, and Nikki came running over. "I'm here. I'm here."

Haze stepped back, as Nikki nudged her out of the way, taking hold of Gabby. "I got here as soon as I could."

"Last push, Gabby." Haze stood by the door, watching as Gabby cried out one last time. "He's here." A few seconds later, they heard the baby's cry. "Would you like to cut the cord?" the midwife asked Nikki. Nikki grinned and did as requested. The baby was cleaned up and placed in Gabby's arms, who silently cried, smiling widely.

"You did it, honey," Nikki said.

"I can't believe he's here."

"He's beautiful, just like his mama."

Gabby turned her head to glance at Nikki, who then bent and kissed Gabby square on the mouth. Haze said nothing. She stood watching the two mothers bond over the birth of their son, knowing she didn't belong there. She backed out through the door, leaving them to it. Despite all the things that were said and done between Gabby and Nikki, the baby's birth changed everything. Gabby might be inclined to give their relationship another chance. Judging by the way Gabby didn't pull back when Nikki kissed her, Haze thought that was possible.

She made her way to her car, started the engine, then headed toward home. It was two in the morning, and all she wanted was a drink. All the shops were shut, so she'd have to make do with the gin in her cupboard. Haze didn't really like liquor, but maybe it would help her forget the image of Gabby and Nikki embracing their new child.

†

He's here. Gabby couldn't believe it. She was propped up in bed, blankets wrapped around her, with her new son cradled in her arms. She was exhausted and couldn't wait to go to sleep, but she couldn't stop smiling at him. She didn't want to miss a second with him. Seven pounds, two ounces. Smaller than she had expected. The birth had gone smoothly and was worth every second of pain to see his cute nose and the fine black hairs coating his head. *Jacob. I love you so much.*

Nicole perched next to her on the mattress, an arm around her shoulders and gazing at Jacob. Her eyes held unshed tears, and her smile matched Gabby's. The only person missing was Haze. Gabby hadn't seen her for the last two hours, since Nicole took her place at Gabby's side. Gabby was a little hurt she hadn't stuck around to meet Jacob.

"Where did Hazel go?" Gabby asked in a whisper, not wanting to disturb the quiet of the room.

"I don't know. I didn't see her leave." Nicole reached out and stroked Jacob's head. "He's gorgeous. Look how small his hand is."

"I know. I can't believe we made him." Gabby glanced at Nicole, smiling.

"Something special to come out of all this."

"What you said tonight, about taking him—"

"Gabby, I'd never do that. He's ours. No matter what happens, he belongs with you. It's not ideal, and I'd love to be with him all the time, but I work too much. It wouldn't be fair."

"So, you'll be okay being a weekend mum?" Gabby hoped with her whole being Nicole was being sincere. If she decided to take him, Gabby would be devastated. Nicole was his biological mother. If she wanted him, she could probably get him. Gabby wasn't sure about the law these days regarding lesbian parenting. Although she was technically a surrogate mother, they had planned to bring the baby up together. Now they were separated, Gabby wasn't sure what that meant. All she knew was how much she loved the little guy and always wanted to be with him.

"It's not what I want, no. But unless you're willing to take me back, it's all I have."

Gabby shook her head and sighed. There was no going back for her, not now she had found Haze. "You can see him whenever you like. I won't keep him from you."

"Are you sure it's over?"

"Nicole, honestly think about what you want and not just the rose-tinted future we saw for ourselves. Can you honestly say you still love me like you used to?"

Nicole looked away for a long moment, her forehead creasing as she frowned. "I wish I did. I really do." She looked back, running her fingers over Gabby's cheek. "I don't know what happened. One day, it just wasn't enough for me anymore." She smiled sadly. "I could see you were falling for Haze. You might not have realised it at the time, but you were."

"I never would have done anything."

"You can't say that for sure."

"I'm sorry, I didn't mean for anything to happen."

Nicole's demeanour shifted. The longing in her gaze was replaced by accusation, and Gabby realised what she had just admitted to

"What do you mean?"

There was no point denying it any longer. Nicole deserved the truth. "We kind of have a thing."

"You've slept with her?"

Nicole leaped from the bed, disturbing Jacob from his sleep. Gabby lifted him onto her shoulder and patted his back. She was too tired for this to become an argument, but she had started it. She may as well continue.

"No, not yet, but we both want to. We've kissed."

"I knew something was going on with you two. When?"

"Yesterday was the first time, but it's been building up for a while now."

Nicole glared at her. "That's why you went to your parents."

"Yes. I didn't know what I wanted."

"So you slept with me to find out?" Nicole's voice had risen. Gabby couldn't blame her, it was a crappy thing to do to her.

"In a way, yes. I didn't mean to hurt you."

"I hurt you first."

"It's not a competition."

"I need to go."

"What? Why?"

"I need to speak to Haze."

"Please, Nicole. It's not her fault. She didn't do anything wrong." Fear swamped Gabby. Judging by the anger rolling off Nicole in waves, Haze would be in for a fight. *I shouldn't have mentioned anything!* "She isn't the reason I don't want to be with you anymore."

"I'll be back later." Nicole grabbed her coat and left, not giving Gabby a chance to stop her.

"Nicole, wait." Gabby reached over to her bag that was on the seat next to her and fished around for her phone. Holding Jacob in one arm, she used her other hand to dial Haze's number. Her stomach dropped when she didn't pick up. She tried again, but it went to voicemail. She shot off a text saying Nicole knew about them and was on her way. She prayed Haze would see it before Nicole arrived.

CHAPTER EIGHTEEN

Haze could hear her phone ringing in the kitchen, but she was too tired, and drunk, to get up and see who it was. She had a good idea it was Gabby. It was nearing four in the morning. No one else would be calling at that hour. Haze still felt bad about leaving without saying goodbye. Watching Nicole and Gabby wrapped up together in their new son was too much. She sipped her gin, pulling a face at the bitter taste. She was on her fifth drink, but the taste hadn't got any better. The phone rang again. She huffed and stood unsteady from the couch, intent on answering. She jumped when the pounding on the front door sounded through the quiet of the house. Haze stumbled over and pulled it wide.

"Nikki? I'd thought you'd still be at the hospital."

"Have you been drinking?"

"Yes."

"Good. Then this might not hurt as much." Nikki pulled back her arm, her fist clenched. Haze didn't have time to register before the punch before it connected with her chin. She fell back against the wall, her hand cradling her face.

"What the fuck was that for?"

Nikki slammed the door. "For kissing my wife."

"She told you?" Haze straightened and followed Nikki into the lounge, keeping her distance to afford her some time if Nikki swung at her again. Being drunk had lowered her reflexes. On any other day, Haze would have put Nikki on her ass.

"About your little love affair? Yes. Although, she said you haven't fucked each other yet. Probably would have been difficult, what with her being so big."

"She isn't big."

Nikki glared at her, but with a condescending smile on her lips. "Oh, you really do love her, don't you?"

There was no point denying it. Nikki had known all along about Haze's feelings. "You know I do."

"What happened to your promises about not going after her? You said you would never do that to me."

"And I didn't. That's why I told her to leave. It was too hard having her here when I couldn't stop loving her."

Nikki stepped toward her, forcing Haze to back up against the wall. "But you went and got her."

"Yes, but only because I missed her so much. I wanted her back as a friend." That much was true. Haze couldn't help it if Gabby loved her back. If Gabby hadn't said so, she would have been content being only her friend.

"But you were supposed to be my mate."

161

"I couldn't get over that you cheated on her, and still are by the looks of things." Haze had no doubt that Nikki had been with Rhea while Gabby was in labour. That could be the only explanation for not getting to the hospital sooner. Even drunk, Haze could clearly remember the state of Nikki's clothes as she burst through the hospital door, all wrinkled and her shirt buttoned wrong. She had obviously dressed in a rush, and it was probably Rhea's room she had dressed in.

"She fell right into your hands, didn't she?" Nikki stepped back and paced the small living room, hands on hips. "I was right about you swooping in the moment you had the chance."

"It wasn't like that."

"At least I cheated with a random woman." Nicole glared at her. "You cheated with your best friend's wife. How low can you get?"

Shame filled Haze, and she studied the carpet. That was the main crux of her guilt. Friends didn't go after each other's wife, certainly not a friend you had known for thirty years. "We haven't done anything." Her voice was barely a whisper. She felt like a child caught doing something wrong.

"You kissed her."

"Only after she said it was over between you."

"You were still my friend," Nikki roared, and Haze flinched. "I hate you for this."

"I'm sorry."

"Sorry enough to not see her again?" Haze looked away. "I didn't think so. I knew all along you had feelings for her, but I stupidly assumed you wouldn't act on it. How naive could I get?"

"I never would have if she went back to you."

"What about now?"

"What?" Haze frowned, struggling to put together Nikki's question.

"Now we're back together. Will you leave us alone?"

"She took you back?" I knew it. I knew they looked too cosy, cooing over the baby. I'm so stupid.

"Yes." Nikki smirked, her eyes looking through Haze. "Having the baby changed everything. We love each other and are going to make it work."

"She wouldn't do that to me," Haze said almost to herself, knowing that wasn't true. Gabby had been undecided for months. Just because she said one thing to Haze, didn't mean she meant it.

"Wouldn't she? You're not so sure, are you? Well, believe me when I say we want nothing to do with you ever again. Leave us alone." Nikki made her way to the door.

"I don't believe you," Haze said in a desperate attempt to get Nikki to admit she was lying.

Nikki turned around, pursing her lips, her eyes calculating. "Has she told you she loves you yet?"

After a moment of hesitation, Haze replied, "No."

"That's right, because she doesn't. She was stringing you along to get back at me for Rhea. She's made her point, and now we're moving on."

"You're lying."

Nikki pulled her phone from her pocket and held it out to Haze. "Call her, ask her." Haze looked at the phone, indecision warring inside her.

"You can't, can you? Because you know it's the truth." She put the phone back in her pocket, a triumphant smile on her face. "You served your purpose. Now it's time to move on and forget all about Gabby. We have a son to concentrate on now. We don't have time for you." She opened the door and stepped through.

"Nikki?"

"What?" Nikki glanced over her shoulder.

"Look after her, okay?"

"Of course I will, she's my wife." With that parting shot, Nikki shut the door, leaving Haze rooted in place in the middle of the lounge. The weight of grief won, and she slumped to her knees, sobs wrenching from her throat. Gabby was gone, back to Nikki. *Would she really do that to me? Lead me on just to get back at Nikki?* Haze leaned back against the couch, head in her hands. Through her muddled mind, she thought of the time they had shared over the last few weeks. The movies they had snuggled in front of, the kiss that got way out of hand, the touching of hands as they cooked together, and the shy smiles. No, Haze couldn't believe all of that was a lie.

She climbed off the floor and went in search of her phone. Three missed calls and a text from Gabby.

Nikki knows about us.

Why would Gabby warn her if it were all a game? Haze opened her Uber app and booked a taxi. She needed to see Gabby.

†

The hour it had taken to wait for the Uber and get to the hospital had sobered Haze up some. She still felt a little off kilter, but the possibility that Gabby never wanted to be with her had driven the buzz away and helped clear her mind. She only had one thing to think about, confronting Gabby and asking if it was true.

She arrived at the maternity ward a little after five thirty. She hoped anyone who saw her would recognise her from the previous night and assume she was there as a new parent. She walked down the long corridor, checking the patient names written in dry marker on the doors as she passed. Finally, she found Gabby's room. She didn't knock. She pushed down the handle and went in. Gabby was sitting in bed, laying back against the pillows, her eyes shut. Her hand rested on the portable cot next to her bed, where the baby slept. Gabby didn't stir until Haze spoke.

"Is it true?"

Gabby's eyes opened, clear and steady but smudged with dark circles. "Haze, where have you been? I've been trying to call you for hours." Haze took a few steps forward, and Gabby's gaze zeroed in on her chin. "Is that a bruise?" Gabby's hand covered her mouth, stifling a gasp. "Oh God, did Nicole do that to you?"

Haze ignored the questions and repeated herself. "Is it true?"

"Is what true?" Gabby flung off the blanket. After glancing at the baby, she swung her legs from the bed. "Did she hurt you?"

"Just tell me if it's true and I'll leave you alone, I promise."

Gabby tried to stand, her hand going to her lower belly. She grimaced and sat back down as if the effort of standing was too much. It probably was. She'd given birth only a few hours ago. "What are you talking about?"

"Was it all just a game?" Haze took another step, Gabby's pull making it hard to stay back. She idly wondered if Gabby always had this power over her. Even after being told it was all a lie, Haze couldn't keep her distance. She couldn't stop the tears that tumbled down her cheeks. "You stringing me along all this time to get back at her."

"What? No." Gabby shook her head, her brows pinching.

"Now the baby's is here, you're back together. You made her suffer but all's okay between you both. You love her. I was just a pawn in your game of revenge." Haze recited the words Nikki had said. Her voice held no emotion, although her heart was breaking. If Gabby confirmed this, she didn't know what she would do.

"Is that what she told you?"

Haze glanced at the hand Gabby held out to her but made no move to take hold. She couldn't, not until she knew the truth. Gabby dropped her hand back to the mattress. "Haze, God, no. How can you believe that? She must know I'd speak to you at some point. Why would she lie to you like that?"

Haze knew why. To get back at her for loving Gabby. To cause as much pain as possible. She had. Haze's insides hadn't stop clenching since Nikki left.

"I told her about us, because she needed to know it's over between her and I for good." Gabby's head tilted to the side, her gaze soft and loving. "I want you, only you."

Haze blinked. "Why?"

"Because I love you."

For the second time that night, Haze slumped to the floor, clutching her knees to her chest. *Could it be true? Does she really love me?* She felt Gabby slide down beside her and circle arms around her in a tight embrace.

"Oh, baby, don't cry."

"She told me it was all a game, that you never wanted me." Haze allowed Gabby to lift her head by the chin and brush her hair back from her eyes.

"I've always wanted you. It just took me so long to figure it out." She lightly traced the bruise on Haze's chin with warm fingers. "I can't believe she would do this to you."

Haze shook her head. "I don't blame her. She's angry."

"We didn't do anything wrong. I'm so sorry she hurt you."

"I'm okay now." She was. Gabby had said the three words Haze had longed to hear for years. She had no choice but to believe her. No other option would do. Gabby was hers now, and she would do everything in her power to keep it that way.

"But you believed her. Why?"

Haze entwined their fingers. "I guess all my insecurities came back up. I've always known you were too good for me. I couldn't understand why you'd want to be with me. When she said it was to make her jealous for cheating on you, it sounded right." Another tear fell. "I'm so sorry."

"Hey, not your fault. I love you, Haze."

"I love you, too."

Just then, the baby cried in his cot. They glanced in his direction. "He's waking up," Gabby said. "Come meet Jacob."

Haze stood and helped Gabby from the cold tile, feeling bad she had caused a scene and made Gabby comfort her just hours after going through childbirth. "Jacob?"

"Nicole's grandfather's middle name." Gabby bent over the cot and lifted him out, placing him in Haze's arms. Haze sat on the bed, cradling Jacob. He wore a tiny cap on his head, his body wrapped tightly in a soft, cotton blanket.

Jacob's eyes opened for only a second, but it was long enough for Haze to fall in love with him. He yawned, poking out his little pink tongue.

"He's so tiny." Haze lowered her head to kiss his cheek.

Gabby sat next to her, with a hand on Haze's thigh. "I felt for sure he'd be an eleven pounder, the size of my belly."

Haze glanced at her. "You weren't that big."

"It felt like it."

"Welcome to the world, Jacob. You're going to break lots of hearts. You're so handsome." Haze was so wrapped up in the emotion of holding him, she didn't hear the door open.

"Get your hands off my child." Nikki's voice was hard and overly loud in the stillness of the room.

"Nicole," Gabby said, shock clear in her tone.

"I said get your hands off him."

Haze handed Jacob back to Gabby, then stood, placing herself in front of Gabby so Nikki couldn't get to her. "I don't want to fight you."

"What part of stay away didn't you get?"

"I can't believe you lied to her." Gabby tucked Jacob back in his cot and stood next to Haze. Taking Haze's hand was a daring move, considering Nikki's clearly visible anger. Haze surmised Gabby was making a stand, showing Nikki they were together and nothing she could do would break them apart.

"I can't believe you want to shack up with that." Nikki tossed a glare at Haze.

"You need to leave."

"No. Not while she's here. That's my son, not yours."

"He's our son, and I'll have whoever I want hold him."

"We'll see about that."

Haze gripped Gabby's hand tighter, holding her back as she started toward Nikki.

"You promised you wouldn't do anything," Gabby pleaded.

"That was before I found out this piece of shit was involved."

The door opened again, a member of the nursing staff glanced at the three of them, her eyebrows furrowing. "What's going on here?"

"She needs to leave." Gabby pointed at Nicole.

"No, I don't. I'm the biological mother." Nicole shoved her finger in Haze's direction. "She's the one who doesn't belong here."

"Please, make her leave," Gabby pleaded.

"Do I need to call security?" the nurse asked, clearly unsure of what was going on.

They all stared at one another, before Nikki finally took a breath. "No. I'm going. This isn't over, Gabby."

Nikki stormed from the room, closely followed by the nurse. Haze turned to Gabby, who sat back on the bed. Her gaze firmly locked on her son, unshed tears wet her eyes.

"Perhaps I should go, too."

"No. I want you to stay." Gabby looked up and reached out her hand. "I need you here."

"Okay." Haze sat beside her.

"We're going to have a fight on our hands, aren't we?"

"I think so." Haze circled Gabby's shoulder with her arm. "I'm sorry. I don't want her to take him from you. Maybe it would be best if we didn't see each other anymore."

"Is that what you want?" Gabby pulled away, staring at her.

"Of course not. I want you and Jacob home with me." Haze looked at the sleeping baby, who was blissfully unaware of what was happening around him. He was only a few hours old and Haze already knew she would do anything to protect him. As much as Haze disliked Nikki just then, Nikki was his mother. Gabby was too. Haze wouldn't be able to bear it if Nicole took him away from Gabby. There was only one option. She wouldn't be the reason Gabby lost her son. "If you being with me will make her fight for him…" She gazed at Gabby, cupping her cheek. "I couldn't do that to you."

"I won't be blackmailed into not seeing you. She can throw all the legal crap in the world at me. I'm not giving you up." Gabby looked at Jacob. "Either of you."

"Are you sure?"

"I love you, Hazel. I need you by my side."

"I need that too."

Gabby smiled, then kissed Haze quickly on the mouth. "Then let's plan on getting out of here and figuring out what we are going to do, together."

"Together."

Haze kissed her again, then cuddled Gabby into her body, keeping her arms wrapped tightly around her. As they watched Jacob sleeping, a multitude of thoughts and feelings competed in her mind. She would do anything to keep Gabby safe and happy. There had to be a way of getting Nikki to agree to not take Jacob. It wasn't fair on Gabby. Yes, maybe starting a relationship with her wasn't the best thing to do right now, but they couldn't keep hiding their feelings for one another. It was going to happen at some point. Haze's arms tightened. She would find a way of making them all happy. There had to be a compromise, for Jacob's sake.

†

That evening, Gabby sat in the armchair in her hospital room, cradling Jacob as she nursed him. Haze had left a few hours earlier to get some rest and would be back soon to take them home. As Gabby watched Jacob suckle, her thoughts traveled to Nicole and her threats to take him. There had to be something she could do that would give her the same rights as Nicole. She wasn't just a surrogate; she had planned to be his mother. To give him up now would be devastating.

Jacob finished feeding, so Gabby pulled her shirt down and lifted him onto her shoulder, rubbing his back. The door opened, and a tired-looking Nicole strolled in. Gabby's heart rate tripled. Has she come to take him?

"Where's your lover?" Nicole narrowed her eyes at Gabby.

"She's not my lover, and she's gone home to get some sleep." Gabby settled Jacob into his cot and covered him with a blanket. She glanced at Nicole. "What are you doing here?"

"I've come to see my son." Nicole walked over to the cot and lifted him back out, holding him against her chest. "And you can't stop me."

Gabby's panic rose, her nerves jangling. If Nicole tried to run, Gabby would give chase, despite her body still being in pain from the birth. She wouldn't let her get away, not with her son. She put her hand in her trouser pocket, fingering her phone. A call to the police would be in order if Nicole tried to take him. "What are we doing, Nicole?"

"I'm holding my baby, and you're shacking up with my best mate."

"That's not fair. We didn't do anything wrong."

"You keep saying that, but you did." Nicole gazed at Jacob as she spoke. "You've had feelings for her all along, haven't you?"

"I didn't think so, but after we separated, yeah, they came to the surface."

"Did you ever love me?" Her voice was so low, Gabby nearly missed the question.

"Of course I did. Nicole, I married you because I loved you. I loved every minute we spent together. I was going to spend my life with you."

"What about Haze?"

"She wasn't in the picture until a few months ago."

Nicole sat in the armchair with Jacob still in her arms. Gabby released a deep breath, feeling less afraid of Nicole running off with him. She moved to stand between Nicole and the door. If she did try to leave, Gabby might have a chance at stopping her.

"But you were always attracted to her?"

There was no point lying. Nicole might as well know the whole truth. "On some level, yes."

"I can't believe this." Nicole glanced up, then back at Jacob. "I won't have her raising my son."

"What did she do that's so bad?"

"She stole my wife," Nicole ground out through gritted teeth.

"No." Gabby wouldn't have Nicole blaming Haze for this. Haze had done nothing for months, despite admitting her feelings. She had done everything in her power to make sure they didn't cross a line, purely because of her friendship with Nicole. If there was any blame to be assigned, it was to Nicole. "You gave me away when you decided to start cheating on me. Who I choose to see is none of your concern now. If that's Haze, it doesn't matter. You and I are through."

Nicole kissed Jacob on the forehead and placed him back in his cot. She turned to face Gabby. "I have a meeting with my solicitor in a couple of days. I'm taking my son, and there is nothing you can do about it."

The words pierced Gabby's flesh like a knife. She's going to take him! "Please, Nicole, you can't do this to me."

"I can, and I will."

"I'm his mother too."

"No, you're just a surrogate." Nicole spat the words with such venom that Gabby wondered if Nicole had ever truly loved her. If she had, how could she do this to her? "And as we're no longer together I can legally take him."

"You said yourself that wouldn't be fair. You're always at work."

"I'll find someone to watch him."

"Why can't that be me?"

Nicole didn't answer.

"Please don't take him from me."

Nicole pointed her finger at Gabby. "You did this. If you had just stayed away from Haze, this wouldn't be an issue."

Gabby had one more defense to make Nicole see she had started this whole thing. "And what about you and Rhea? You're the one who cheated, not me."

"Rhea is just a bit of fun, something I no longer got from you."

"Is a bit of fun?" Gabby narrowed her eyes, her suspicions confirmed. "You're still seeing her?"

Nicole looked away. "That's none of your concern."

"Why did it take you so long to get here when I went into labour? You were with her, weren't you? You dropped me off, then went straight to her after you proposed to me."

Nicole shrugged. "So what? You didn't want me anyway."

"What if I had said yes? Would you have still gone to see her?" Nicole shrugged again as if she didn't see anything wrong with her behaviour. *You can't propose one minute, then go sleep with someone else.* "You're disgusting. I can't believe how cold you've gotten."

"To quote your words, who I see is of no concern to you. All that matters is keeping my son away from Haze."

"Why do you hate her so much? What has she ever done to you?"

"She took my wife."

"A wife you cheated on!" *Why can't she see this?* "We had every right to pursue things. You and I were over."

"And I have every right to keep my son." She kissed Jacob one last time and strode to the door. "You'll be hearing from my solicitor."

Gabby walked heavily over to the chair. She lowered herself slowly, her body tense. Nothing she said had made any difference. Nicole was determined to take him. *Maybe giving up Haze is the best thing to do.* She gazed at Jacob. *If leaving her will keep my son, that's what I should do.* No, she couldn't do that. She loved Haze too much to throw away a chance at a life with her. *But I can't lose him.* The weight of the situation crushed her. How could she choose between the two? She couldn't. She just had to hope she had some legal rights to be his mother, even if that meant only seeing him weekends. None of this mess was ideal. Her plan to be with Nicole and raise a family had been obliterated.

Gabby would need to gather as much of the smashed pieces as she could. She would have a future with Haze and Jacob, in whatever form that took.

So wrapped up in her thoughts, she didn't hear the door open and Haze walking in. Haze's face came into focus as she knelt beside her, concern in her gaze.

"Gabby? Are you okay?"

"Nicole was just here. She still wants to take Jacob." Her voice was flat, no emotion, resigned to the fact Nicole hated them so much she was willing to tear them all apart.

"I'm so sorry."

"How can she do this to me?"

"I don't know, sweetheart."

"She's seeing her solicitor in a couple of days. I guess I'd better contact one as well." Gabby's eyes filled with tears. "What do I do if she takes him? He's my boy."

Haze brushed the tears away with her thumb. "We'll figure something out, I promise. Are you ready to come home?"

"Yes. I just need to be discharged and arrange when the midwife will be coming to visit next."

"Okay. Let's get him in the car seat and ready to go." Haze stood and placed the car seat Gabby hadn't noticed onto the bed.

"Haze?"

"Yeah?"

"I don't know what I would do without you."

"You never have to find out." Haze smiled and kissed her cheek.

Grief and fear held Gabby to her seat. Haze made baby noises at Jacob, as she bundled him into the car seat. Her love for him was as clear as Gabby's own. *Why didn't I wait to get pregnant? This would all be so much better if Haze and I had gotten pregnant together. There was no point dwelling on the what-ifs. Jacob is here now and I wouldn't change that for the world, no matter how many threats Nicole makes.*

CHAPTER NINETEEN

Haze jolted up in bed, unsure of what had awoken her. As far as she could recall, she hadn't been dreaming. She listened to the sounds of the house, hearing nothing but silence. Perhaps Jacob woke up. They had driven home from the hospital in silence. Haze had tried to bring Gabby out of her low mood, but after stilted, one-word answers, Haze gave up. She hated Nikki for what she was putting Gabby through. She could understand Nikki was upset by their recent pairing, but she had no right to lay blame on Gabby and take Jacob away from her. It wasn't fair. Haze didn't think Gabby would ever be able to get over losing him.

She strained her ears but still heard nothing. She laid back down just as she heard a quiet sob coming from down the hall. Haze threw off her duvet and went in search of

177

Gabby. The door to her room was ajar. Jacob's night light glowed softly in the darkness. Haze pushed the door wider and stepped through. Gabby was sitting in the rocking chair, Jacob cradled in her arms. A few tears rolled down Gabby's cheek, as she gazed at her son.

"Gabby? It's three o'clock in the morning. What are you doing?" Haze crossed over to her and knelt, lightly tracing Jacob's head. Gabby didn't look her way. If she hadn't spoken, Haze would have thought Gabby didn't know she was there.

"He woke up for a feed about twelve. I couldn't put him back down. I don't know how much longer I might have with him. I guess I wanted to hold him for as long as possible, in case I don't get another chance."

"Gabby, sweetheart, we're going to figure something out." Haze reached up and cupped Gabby's cheek, noting how cold her skin felt. "We've booked in to see a solicitor next week. We'll find a way to keep him."

Gabby glanced at her for only a second. "But what if we can't? What if I have to give him up?"

"I don't know, sweetheart. I can't answer that." Haze dropped her hand, feeling impotent in Gabby's plight. She didn't know what to say. She could promise it was all going to be alright, but they both knew those were empty words. Haze had no idea what was going to happen. She couldn't predict the future. "I'm here for you, always."

"I know." Gabby smiled. "That's what makes this whole thing bearable." She shook her head. "How can someone we both loved do this to us?"

"I wish I knew. I never would have thought she'd turn out the way she has, but there's nothing we can do about her now. We need to fight, and to fight you need your rest."

Haze stood and took Jacob from Gabby's unwilling hands. She ignored Gabby's glare and placed him in his cot, making sure he was tucked up tight. She held out her hand. "Come with me." Gabby took her hand, and Haze led them to the bed. She pulled back the cover and climbed inside, holding her arms open for Gabby.

Gabby gazed longingly at Haze. "We haven't really shared a bed before."

"I know."

"I'm not ready for anything."

Even in the muted light, Haze could see Gabby's endearing blush. "I'm not asking for anything. I just want to hold you while you sleep. Is that okay?"

"It's everything." Gabby climbed in and pulled the blanket over them. Haze wrapped her arms around her, resting Gabby's head on her chest. "Thank you."

"No problem."

"I love how safe I feel in your arms." Gabby's fingers began to dance over Haze's stomach through the fabric of the tank top she wore. Her stomach clenched. "Is it wrong of me to be glad she cheated?" Gabby asked. She looked up, into Haze's eyes. "Because of that, I can now be here with you."

"No, it's not wrong. I'm glad too. Although I've lost a friend, I've gained so much more." Haze paused for a moment. "If it hadn't happened, I would have been fine just being your friend."

Gabby grinned. "Liar."

"Okay, it would have sucked. I think that's why I distanced myself from you guys over the last year. Knowing you were having her baby nearly drowned me. I couldn't bear to be on the outside watching you with her." The day Nikki had told her they were pregnant was the day Haze knew her love would always be unrequited. It was different when Gabby and Nikki were only dating. Haze could always dream they'd break up and Gabby would come running. As the years passed and their relationship progressed, Haze pulled further away from them. Their movie nights dwindled, day trips were cancelled, and phone calls were few and far between. It was just too hard for Haze to see them so happy. She loved that she was now holding Gabby, but she would give anything to take away Gabby's hurt.

"I did wonder why we hadn't seen you as much. I'm sorry you were in so much pain."

"It's okay. You know I'd give anything to make all of this go away, right?"

"I know, and that's why I love you."

"Get some sleep. He'll be wanting to feed again soon."

"Will you stay?"

"For as long as you need me to."

"Forever?"

"If that's what you want." She'd do anything for Gabby, even leave if Gabby asked her to, no matter how much it would crush her.

"I do."

"Then I'll be here. I love you, Gabby."

Haze kissed Gabby's forehead, then closed her eyes. *Tomorrow, I'll go see Nikki, talk to her, try to make her see sense.* Hurting Gabby this way wasn't right, and Haze vowed to do whatever it took to get things back to how they should be.

†

Haze had been awake for an hour. She was loath to disturb Gabby, who still slept peacefully beside her. Jacob had woken them once. Gabby fed him on the bed, with Haze looking on. It was a magical moment to see mother and son bond. After he was finished, Haze returned him to his cot and crawled back in bed beside Gabby. They were in the same position when Haze woke up. She took that time to think about what she was going to say to Nikki. She doubted reasoning with her would work. Nikki hated them now. For all Haze knew, talking to her might just make the situation worse. As if sensing Haze was watching her, Gabby's eyelids fluttered open. She smiled when she saw Haze gazing at her.

"Good morning," Gabby murmured, snuggling in closer to Haze.

"Hey. How are you feeling this morning?"

"A lot better." Gabby grinned, her fingers brushing back Haze's hair. "I think it has something to do with the excellent sleep I had last night."

"Yeah?"

"Yeah. Thank you for being there for me."

"Always." Haze leaned in and kissed her gently, lingering on her lips but not attempting to deepen the kiss. She pulled back. "Maybe we can do it again tonight?"

"I'd like that. What do you have planned for today?"

"I need to make a start on Sandy's website and send out some invoices." Haze cleared her throat, hating she was about to tell a white lie to Gabby. "I, uh, also need to make a run into town to pick up some supplies."

"Busy day then?"

"Not too busy. I'll still have plenty of time to spend with you and Jacob."

"Sounds great." Gabby kissed Haze's neck, then sat up and glanced over at Jacob, who still slept soundly. "I need to call my parents to give them an update. I was also thinking of seeing if Edith wanted to come over for coffee, meet the baby."

"Cool. I'm going to go into town in a minute, get it out of the way before the roads get too busy. Do you need anything while I'm gone?"

"I don't think so, thanks."

"No problem." Haze rose from the bed and lifted Jacob from the cot. She nestled him on the bed with Gabby. "I'm going to get dressed and make a move. I'll see you in a little while."

Gabby smiled, as she tickled Jacob's hand. "We'll miss you. Bye."

"See you later." Haze bent at the waist, kissing Gabby, then Jacob. "Bye, handsome. Look after Mummy."

Thirty minutes later, Haze was strolling through the lobby of Nikki's building. She took the elevator up to the eighth floor and headed for Nikki's office. She peeked inside, finding it empty. She looked around and spotted someone she assumed was Nikki's assistant.

"Where can I find Nicole?"

"She's in the conference room holding a meeting."

"Thanks." Haze crossed over the floor to where she knew the conference room was, the assistant trailing after her.

"You can't go in there," the assistant said, as Haze pushed open the door.

"I don't care." She stepped over the threshold. Twelve sets of eyes all glared in her direction. "Nikki, we need to talk."

Nikki stood forcibly from her chair, her face turning red. She leaned her hands on the table and stared at Haze, her jaw working but no words being spoken. Eventually, she sighed and glanced at her colleagues.

"Excuse me, everyone. I need to take care of this." Nikki stormed past Haze in the direction of her office. Haze quickened her step and followed. She had come to talk to Nikki peacefully. Barging in on her meeting was probably not the smartest thing to do. Once inside the office, Nikki slammed the glass door with such force Haze wondered how it didn't shatter.

"What do you think you're doing coming here and interrupting my meeting?"

"I need to talk to you."

"Couldn't it have waited?" Nikki's gaze glanced at Haze's chin. "Or were you looking for another bruise to match that one?"

Haze lifted her hands up, palms facing forward. "I don't want to fight. We need to talk about Jacob."

"He is no concern of yours."

"You're wrong. It concerns Gabby, so he concerns me too."

Nikki turned her back, then proceeded to sit at her desk and open a file, obviously in an attempt to dismiss Haze. No, not this time. "Please, Nikki. Just hear me out."

Nikki sighed and flipped the file shut. "Fine. Take a seat."

Haze sat but didn't speak. For all her bravado in coming, now she was faced with Nikki, she didn't know what to say.

"Well?"

Time to lay it all out. Haze took a breath. "I know you're upset and hurt that Gabby and I are together."

"Understatement." Nikki rolled her eyes.

"Is it really that bad?"

"My best friend and my wife?" She let out a sarcastic laugh. "Yeah, it's that bad."

"It's not ideal, no. But you two were done. It'll take some time, but you'll get over it."

"Will I?"

"Yes."

Nikki sat back in her chair, gently swaying it side to side as she thought. "You're probably right. Doesn't mean I have to like it."

"So why punish Gabby by taking Jacob?"

The swinging stopped. Nikki fixed her with a powerful stare. "He's my son."

"He's hers too. You know that. Last night I walked into her room. She was holding him and crying. She had been there for hours, just looking at him. She's devastated to think she might not get many more chances to be with him. You're breaking her heart, again. It's not right, and you know it."

"So what, you expect me to sit back while you play happy families with my kid?" She shook her head. "I don't think so."

"We can all be involved." Haze leaned forward in her chair, wanting Nikki to see how serious she was, and desperate. "You don't have to be left out. You're his mother. You can both raise him. You don't need to take him away because you're angry with us. He deserves to be loved by as many people as possible. All you're doing is hurting him and hurting Gabby. That isn't you. I've known you your whole life. You've never done something so cruel in all that time."

Nikki looked away, chewing her lip. "You're right, I haven't." She scowled at Haze. "But then I haven't been fucked over before, by the people I trusted most in the world."

"Not to lay blame, but you fucked her over first. None of this would have happened if you hadn't slept with bimbo barbie."

"Don't call her that." Nicole's voice held a note of warning that set alarm bells off in Haze's head.

"Oh my God. You have feelings for her, don't you?"

"Of course not."

"You do. I've seen that look before. You had the same when you first met Gabby."

"So what if I do?" Nikki shrugged.

"When? When did you fall for her?"

Nikki didn't answer for a long moment, but then she blew out a breath. "The first time I saw her when she moved to my division. I couldn't help it. I could see how much Gabby liked you, and I felt neglected. Rightly or wrongly, that's how I felt. When Rhea moved over, I couldn't stop myself from liking her."

All this time you were trying to get back with Gabby but you were already in love with someone else? Haze couldn't get her mind around it. Why try and fight for Gabby if she had her sights set on Rhea? "If you love someone else, why are you being like this?" For the first time in a long while, Haze saw true sadness in Nikki's features.

"You were my best friend, Haze. I trusted you. Yeah, maybe I am to blame for all this, but it still hurts to know you and she are together."

"So you're hurting Gabby because I hurt you? You do realise that's dumb."

"Maybe."

"Hate me all you want, but think about Gabby. She doesn't deserve this. You can work something out. I know you can. Please, Nikki. If she ever meant anything to you, please don't take him away from her."

Nikki's shoulders heaved as she took a deep breath. "I'll think about it."

"That's all I ask."

"You'd better go." Nikki motioned to the door with a flick of her head.

"Okay." Haze stood. "Nikki, I really am sorry about all this."

"Are you? You got what you wanted."

Haze shook her head. "I never wanted it to be this way. You know that." Nikki stared at her a long while before nodding.

"Yeah, I do. Goodbye, Haze."

"Goodbye, Nikki."

As Haze made her way back to her car, she couldn't help thinking that was a final goodbye between friends. Despite Nikki being with Rhea, she obviously couldn't get over that Haze had gone for Gabby. *Perhaps that's why she tried so hard to win her back, to stop me from having her. Well, it doesn't matter now.* Gabby was with Haze, and Haze planned to keep it that way for as long as she could.

She got in her car and drove to the local stationery shop, just so she had something to take home. She didn't want to tell Gabby she had been to see Nikki, just in case it was for naught. She prayed Nikki had listened to what she said and would do what was right for them all.

†

Gabby clicked the last popper in place on Jacob's baby grow, then wrapped him in a soft lilac blanket. She had just finished giving him his bath, and he looked all warm and cosy. She hugged him to her shoulder with one arm and used her other hand to throw away his nappy in the bin next to the changing table. Gabby couldn't believe how fast their first week had gone. She was still sore and exhausted, but every time she looked at Jacob, her heart filled with overwhelming love and joy that washed away all her fatigue.

She carried him down the hallway and into the lounge, where Haze was sprawled on the couch, working on her laptop. She looked up as Gabby approached and made room on the sofa for her. Gabby settled next to her, Jacob in her arms. Haze reached over and smoothed his head.

"Did he enjoy his bath?" Haze stroked his hand that poked out from the blanket. Gabby smiled at Haze's enthusiasm over Jacob. She had been amazing this past week. Although Gabby was the only one who could feed Jacob, Haze still got up with her and helped settled him after he finished. She even changed his nappies. For someone who never wanted children, Haze was amazing with him. Gabby's smile dimmed, as she realised Nicole still wanted to take him. They hadn't heard from her all week, so Gabby prayed she had changed her mind.

"He's a little young to understand what's going on around him," Gabby replied, smiling at the goofy face Haze was pulling for Jacob, whose eyes were open. It was cute, considering Jacob wouldn't be able to see her clearly, but it warmed Gabby's heart just the same. She hoped Jacob would be seeing them both for a long time to come.

"Nah, I bet he thought it was just like floating in Mummy."

"At least this time when he kicked his legs, he wasn't bashing my insides around."

"He's so cute."

"Let's hope he stays that way."

A knock on the front door cut off Haze's reply. It was nearing eight at night. Who would be visiting so late in the evening? Her heart rate increased when she figured it could only be one person. Nicole. Gabby's arms involuntarily held Jacob tighter.

"I'll get it." Haze rose from the couch and opened the door. Gabby didn't miss the stiffening of her back. "Nikki."

"Is now a good time to talk?"

"Sure, come on in." Haze stepped aside, allowing Nicole to enter.

"Gabby."

"Hello." Gabby rose, trying not to let fear overwhelm her as Nicole came closer, then peered down at Jacob.

"Can I hold him?" Nicole glanced up at Gabby.

"Of course." Going against her better judgment, Gabby handed him over with sweating palms. "He's just had a bath, so he smells really good."

Nicole took Jacob and sat in the armchair. "Hello, Jacob. You've gotten so big already." She tilted her head down and kissed his cheek. "I missed you."

"Can I get you a drink or anything?" Haze came to stand by Gabby's side. Her presence helped steady Gabby's nerves. If Nicole wanted to take him, she would have to get past Haze first. Gabby had no doubt Haze would stop her.

"No thanks. I won't stay long. I've got some work still to do back at the office. I've been doing a lot of thinking since Haze came to see me."

188

Gabby studied Haze, her brows furrowing. *You kept that quiet.* "You went to see her?"

"Yes. I'm sorry I didn't tell you, but I didn't want you to be upset."

Gabby drew in a breath, clearing her initial anger from her body. Haze had only ever tried to support Gabby. If she went to go see Nicole it was for a very good reason. "It's okay." Gabby smiled briefly, then focused back on Nicole. "What have you come up with?"

"This isn't easy for me," Nicole started, shaking her head. "I've made a lot of mistakes. I hurt you terribly, and I'm sorry. But seeing you two together...I guess all along I knew you were better suited with each other."

"Nicole, I loved you."

"I know you did. But with Haze, it's stronger, like you were meant to be together. I'm not happy about it, but that's my issue to deal with. Haze made me realise that separating you from Jacob isn't fair. He's your son just as much as mine."

Gabby couldn't believe her ears. Was Nicole really saying she wanted to allow Jacob to stay here? She tried not to let her hopes rise to much. Nicole had said the same before and had changed her mind. She could do the same again. "What are you saying?"

"I've spoken to my solicitor. He told me if both our names are on the birth certificate, we both get equal parenting rights. He would legally be yours. So that's what we'll do." Still holding Jacob, Nicole reached into her pocket and withdrew an envelope. She handed it to Gabby, who reached for it with trembling fingers. "I know you don't trust me right now, so I got a notarised letter detailing this arrangement. I don't want you to think I'll change my mind again."

Gabby clutched the envelope to her chest, tears filling her eyes. Jacob would be staying; she would be his mother. "Thank you so much."

"Now the merger is complete, I should be able to have a more flexible schedule. I'd like to see him as much as I can."

"Any time you want, just let me know."

"Thank you. I was hoping I could take him Friday night and Saturday, once he's no longer breastfeeding of course."

"That's fine with me.

"As much as I'd like to see him all the time, I know the hours I work won't permit it. That's why he should stay with you."

Gabby needed to make sure this was really happening, that Nicole really wanted it to be this way. She didn't think she could handle it if Nicole reversed her decision again. Until the birth certificate was in place, Gabby would need to play by Nicole's rules, and she didn't like that. "Are you sure about this?"

"Yes. It pains me to admit it, but I know you'll take better care of him."

Gabby shook her head. "That's not true. You'll be a wonderful mother."

"Thanks for saying that, but you've always been the more maternal one." Nicole glanced between Gabby and Haze, her throat working as she swallowed hard a few times. "There's something else. As Haze never told you she came to see me, there's something you won't know. Rhea and I are dating. There's no commitment at the moment, but she means a lot to me."

Jacob began to fuss. Nicole handed him over to Gabby, who patted his back and rocked him gently. "I don't understand. If you had feelings for her, why try so hard to win me back?"

"I don't know. I guess I didn't want to admit we were over. You know I hate failure."

"Can you put him down for me?" Gabby passed Jacob to Haze, who took him and headed down the hallway. Gabby turned her attention back to Nicole. "Does she make you happy?"

"Yes."

"Then congratulations." Gabby was stunned, to say the least. She had always assumed Nicole was just out for more scx. She had no idea feelings were involved. In a way, it made the betrayal a little easier to deal with. Knowing she cheated on her with someone she had feelings for was more tolerable then screwing for the sake of screwing. Gabby couldn't find it in herself to be angry with her, after all, the affair had paved the way for her to be with Haze.

"Same question to you, does Haze make you happy?"

Gabby nodded. "She does. I'm sorry."

"No, don't apologise. I still hate the idea, but you can make your own choices now."

"We never meant to hurt you," Gabby replied, just as Haze reentered the lounge.

"I know, it would have happened at some point anyway. You have too much chemistry to ignore forever."

Haze spoke before Gabby could. "I never would have done—"

"Stop saying that, Haze. I know you wouldn't have. It still hurts just the same. I don't think I can see you for a while. Maybe one day, we can put this all behind us. For now, I just can't."

Haze nodded. "I understand."

"Right, I should go." Nicole stood and headed for the door. She glanced down the hallway toward the bedroom, as if expecting to see Jacob waving at her from the doorway. "I'll see you soon, little man," she whispered.

"Thank you, Nicole. You have no idea how much this means to me."

"Yeah, I do. Look after him, okay?"

"I will."

"Would it be okay if I came by Wednesday after work?"

"Of course."

"Okay. Goodnight."

"Goodnight." Haze closed the door behind Nicole, and they both slumped back onto the couch. "Well, that was unexpected. I can't believe she changed her mind. What did you say to her?"

Haze took her hand, leaning down to kiss her fingers. "Just that it wasn't fair to punish you because we're together. I think she realised how cruel that was."

"And Rhea? I thought they were just having sex."

"Me too. She said she liked her when Rhea started working for her office."

"So it wasn't just sex, she actually had an affair with her."

"Does that upset you?" Haze asked from behind lowered lashes.

"I guess I can't be too mad at her." Gabby tilted up Haze's head by her chin so she could see her eyes. "I did fall for you."

"Yeah, but that was after you broke up. She had an affair while you were still together."

"I don't think it matters now who's in the wrong. It's been a difficult four months, but it's all over now. We've both moved on, and we have Jacob. It's time to put it behind us."

Haze leaned over and kissed Gabby on the lips. Pulling back she asked, "Do you think she'll always hate me?"

There was no point lying to Haze. Throughout this whole mess, it was Haze's and Nicole's friendship that had been ruined the most. Gabby was fine not being with Nicole, and Nicole was obviously happy with Rhea. It was only Haze that had been put in the middle and lost. "It's a possibility. Will you be okay with not being friends?"

"In time, yeah. But right now, it hurts. I'm still pissed she hurt you, so I can't be upset she hates me. Thirty years is a long time to be friends with someone." Gabby glanced away, wrestling with her guilt. "I know what you're thinking, and no, I don't want to lose you either. If my friendship with Nikki can't be repaired, then so be it. I'm not giving you up, not now I've got you."

"It'll all work out in the end." Gabby reached over and brushed her fingers through Haze's hair, then cupped her cheek.

"I hope so. I love you Gabby."

"And I love you." Gabby glanced down at Haze's lips. "I can't wait to make love to you."

"Yeah?" Haze did a deliberate scan of Gabby's body with her eyes, causing Gabby to flush. "When do you think you'll be all healed down there?" She smirked, waggling her eyebrows.

Gabby grinned. "Not for a while, so you'll just have to wait."

Haze turned serious. "I've waited ten years for you, a few weeks won't kill me."

Jacob's cry sounded from the bedroom. "Dinner time again." Gabby reluctantly let go of Haze and stood.

"Shall I order us some food as well?"

"That would be nice. Anything is fine." Gabby entered the bedroom and scooped Jacob up. She settled in the rocking chair and lifted her top. Jacob immediately started suckling. Breastfeeding was a strange experience at first, but now Gabby loved the feeling of bonding with him like this. She couldn't stop the few tears that fell as she recalled Nicole's visit. Jacob was hers and she had Haze. All was going to work out. She imagined things would be awkward between Haze and Nicole when she came over to visit Jacob, but she hoped things would eventually settle down and they could all be one big happy family. As long as Jacob was healthy and loved, Gabby could take on anything else.

CHAPTER TWENTY

"Have you got everything?" Gabby asked, as Nicole picked up Jacob's car seat in one hand and a rucksack in the other. Gabby had packed two changes of clothes, nappies, wet wipes, four bottles of breast milk she had expressed that day, and the stuffed bear Haze had bought Jacob. Nicole was having him overnight for the first time, and Gabby couldn't stop herself from worrying. She didn't fear Nicole would keep him. The last four weeks had proved that Nicole was serious about Gabby having him full time.

This was the first time they'd be apart. She had spent every minute with Jacob since his birth, and she couldn't stop herself from missing him. *He's not even gone yet, and I miss him so much already.*

"I think so." Nicole smiled at her. "Gabby, it's only for one night. We'll be back bright and early, first thing."

"You'll call if you need anything?"

"Of course."

"And you have enough milk?"

Nicole's smile widened. "If not, I'll come and get some. Gabby, relax. I know you're worried, but I'll be fine."

Gabby blew out a breath and tried to release her tight muscles. Relaxing was easier said than done. Her whole world was bundled up in a car seat and about to leave the house. "It's just this is the first time away from him. I'm not sure I'm ready."

"Are you worried I might not be able to cope?" Nicole looked hurt.

"No, you'll be fine, but what if he needs me?"

"Then we'll come back. It's not forever, just a few hours. Enjoy the respite while you can. He'll be home in no time."

"And you're sure you'll be alright?"

"He's a baby, how hard can it be? Besides, I'm looking forward to bonding with him."

"He hasn't been on the bottle long, so he might fuss at first." As much as Gabby loved the feeling of feeding Jacob herself, she knew Nicole was desperate to spend time with him on her own. For that to happen, Gabby needed to stop breastfeeding. It wouldn't be fair to Nicole to keep him on the nipple for months.

"Gabby, stop worrying."

"I can't."

"I know. I'll send you plenty of updates."

"Okay." Gabby bent and kissed Jacob, gently smoothing his head with the back of her fingers. She bit her lip as tears filled her eyes. "Be a good boy for your mama."

"Have a nice evening."

"You too."

Gabby pulled open the door and watched as Nicole put Jacob in the car and then pulled away. Her heart broke as the car disappeared around the corner. It's just one night. We'll both be fine. She closed the door and glanced at the clock. Haze would be home from her meeting any minute. Time to get everything ready. With the house to themselves for the first time in weeks, Gabby wanted to do something nice for Haze to say thank you for all her help. She started the bath and squirted in some bubbles. She grabbed a couple of candles from the lounge, lit them, and placed them around the edge of the tub. She also fetched the chilled champagne from the fridge and grabbed a glass, setting them on the closed toilet seat. Just as the bath finished filling, Haze's voice called from the hallway.

"Gabby? Are you home?"

Gabby slipped from the bathroom, closing the door behind her, and went to greet Haze. "Hello, sweetheart." She wrapped her arms around Haze's neck and kissed her deeply, loving the feel of Haze pulling her tight into her body. Gabby had been worried her libido may have dwindled since giving birth, but Haze's hands roaming over her back ignited a fire in her stomach. She just hoped when it came time to show Haze her body, Haze wouldn't be horrified with all the stretch marks and loose skin below her belly button.

Gabby pulled back and grinned at Haze's hooded eyes and flushed cheeks, pleased Haze appeared to be as excited as she was. "Come with me." Gabby pulled her along to the bathroom and ushered her inside. Haze took in the bubble bath and candles in one long look, then turned to Gabby.

"What's all this?"

"You've done a great job in looking after Jacob and me, so I thought I'd repay the favour."

"You don't need to do that. You're my family."

Gabby smiled. "I know, but still. Take your clothes off and climb in." Gabby turned her back to give her some privacy, resisting the urge to glance into the bathroom mirror in the hopes of catching Haze with nothing on. *All in good time, Gabby.*

"Where's Jacob?"

"Nicole has him for the night."

"What? Why?"

"It's time they started to bond properly." Gabby waited till she heard Haze step into the water, then she turned around. Thankfully the bubbles hid everything. She wanted Haze to enjoy the treat, not be gawked at. "I want him to know she's his mother, not just a visitor. She wants that too."

"Why didn't you tell me?"

"Because I wanted to surprise you." Gabby picked up the glass and poured the bubbly liquid. "Champagne?"

"Thank you."

Gabby bent and kissed Haze's forehead. "You relax for a bit, while I go make sure the other part of your surprise is ready."

"There's more?"

"Yes. Close your eyes and relax."

Gabby closed the bathroom door and headed into the bedroom. She lit the multitude of candles she'd positioned around the room and turned off the light. Then she turned on the CD player, soft piano music filled the air. She pulled off the duvet, folding it and placing it on the floor. With everything ready, she sat on the mattress and waited for Haze. While she did so, she texted Nicole quickly to make sure everything was okay. Her reply was a photo of Jacob sleeping in her arms. It was clear someone else had taken the photo. Gabby wondered if it was Rhea, then realised it didn't really matter. Nicole was entitled to have whomever she wanted over.

Twenty minutes later Haze called out. "Gabby?"

"In the bedroom."

Haze opened the door, her gaze instantly finding Gabby. "Wow. That's a lot of candles."

"I think it sets the mood perfectly."

"You're right."

Gabby stood and smiled nervously. She wasn't intending to seduce Haze. The ends of her hair were wet against skin tinged a light pink from the heat of the bath. Gabby's desire for Haze took off all on its own. She wanted to make love to her, but first, she would give her the massage she'd planned. "Take off your robe and lie face down on the bed."

"I'm naked under here."

Gabby smirked. "And?"

"Okay." Haze shrugged, then untied the sash. The robe dropped from her shoulders. Gabby swallowed hard, as every glorious inch of Haze's body came into view. Her skin was flawless, smooth and tight. Haze lifted one side of her mouth into a half grin, then draped herself over the bed. Gabby took a breath and climbed up, putting one knee either side of Haze's thighs. She ran her fingers gently over Haze's back, loving the soft feel of her skin. She felt her shiver.

"What are you doing?" Haze murmured.

"I'm giving you a massage."

"You're giving me a heart attack."

Gabby chuckled and moved her hands lower, tickling the rounded edges of Haze's ass. Haze bucked her hips slightly. "How about now?"

"Jesus, Gabby."

"Turn over." Gabby rose up to allow Haze to roll over, her gaze went to Haze's perfect breasts, her nipples already tight and stiff. "You have a very nice body, Haze. I've been wanting to touch you forever."

"You only had to ask."

"I'm asking now."

"Touch away."

Gabby started at Haze's collarbones, running her fingers down her biceps, then back up. Her fingers roamed over her chest, inching ever closer to Haze's breasts. Finally, her hands cupped her, erect nipples digging into her palms. Gabby squeezed, her own hips pressing hard into Haze's thighs. She felt herself grow wet, her pulse pounding hard. "I want to make love to you, but I'm afraid you'll be disappointed."

Haze frowned. "In what?"

Gabby looked away, her hands stilling. "Pregnancy has changed a lot of things."

"You're ashamed about your body? Gabby, that's crazy. You're beautiful." Gabby stared at the wall, fearing she'd cry. "Look at me." Haze cupped her cheek, turning her head. Haze's gaze was fierce, electrifying Gabby to her core. "You're beautiful, Gabby. A few stretch marks won't change that."

"My breasts are saggy," she whispered.

"If you think I care for one moment about how perky your boobs are, then you're nuts. Gabby, your body gave Jacob his life. Your breasts feed him to help him grow. Your heart loves him more than anything. Your soul would die if you lost him. Everything you are provides him with nourishment. That's the most beautiful thing in the world a mother can do for their child. And right now, the only thing I can concentrate on is the fact I need to come soon because your hips are driving me crazy." Gabby hadn't realised her hips were still grinding on Haze. "So stop worrying and let me make love to you."

"I love you, Hazel."

Haze didn't reply. She reached up and pulled Gabby down, so their bodies were flush together. Haze kissed her, and before Gabby knew what was happening, Haze had stripped off her T-shirt and bra and was working on the button of her trousers. All of Gabby's insecurities fled the moment she felt Haze's fingers trace her stomach then move lower between her thighs. The first touch of fingertips to her clit made her flinch then surge into Haze. This was everything. For weeks she had waited for this, for Haze to claim her, to unify their bodies as one. Being with Haze was exquisite. Before too long, her orgasm crested and left her trembling in Haze's arms.

"That was incredible," Haze whispered into Gabby's hair.

"I never thought I would feel so much all at once. It's never been like that before." Gabby leaned up, gazing into Haze's eyes. "You're so intense, passionate. I didn't worry about my body at all. The moment you touched me, all I could think about was you."

"Good." Haze kissed her quickly, her hand cupping Gabby's ass. "That's the way it should be."

"I never want to lose this feeling."

"We won't, I promise."

Gabby was about to lean into another kiss, but her mobile beeped from the nightstand. She reached over and grabbed the phone. "It's a picture message from Nicole. Jacob is fast asleep."

"You seem disappointed."

"No, not at all." She sent off a text then put her phone down. "It's just…I don't know. I thought he'd miss me more." *Isn't it good he's settled instead of screaming for me?*

"He knows he's safe and secure. I'm sure he does miss you, but he probably recognises Nikki."

"That's a good thing, right?"

"Yes."

Gabby snuggled back into Haze's arms. "I don't think I'll ever be okay with him out of the house."

"And that's what makes you an excellent mother. Now, don't worry about Jacob, he's fine. We have an urgent matter to attend to."

"And what would that be?"

"My burning desire for you. I've waited so long for you. Now I've had you, I want you all the time."

"Then take me, I'm yours."

"If you insist."

Their lovemaking carried on into the night, sometimes fast, sometimes slow and deliberate. Gabby felt loved and cared for, more than she ever had in her life. The idle thought of why it hadn't been this way with Nicole floated through her mind, but she decided it didn't matter. Her life with Nicole was different from her life with Haze. She had been happy and satisfied with Nicole. With Haze, she felt those things, but also a hot burning passion she hadn't thought she could ever feel. Haze brought that out of her. Perhaps Nicole was right when she said they would have gotten together at some point anyway; the chemistry really was that strong between them. Everything was working out for them all, Nicole included. As far as Gabby knew, she was still seeing Rhea. Nicole seemed more settled, happy within herself, and Gabby was glad for her. Things were still strained between Haze and Nicole, but they were always civil with each other when Nicole came over to see Jacob. Only the passage of time might one day heal the hurt they both felt. For now, Haze was happy, Gabby was happy, and life had never been sweeter.

Epilogue

Haze's hand flew over the page as she added more shading to the drawing. She was in the garden, sat at the wooden table, sketching Gabby and Jacob as they slept in the shade of the umbrella Haze had wedged into the grass. Jacob was eight months old. Haze couldn't believe how fast he was growing. Light reflecting off her ring finger made her smile. Two weeks earlier, Gabby had cooked a romantic meal, then proceeded to get down on one knee. The proposal was a shock. The last few months had been good. Nicole was living with Rhea, and seemingly in love. Their routine hadn't taken long to settle into. Although Gabby was a little wary of Rhea, she liked how much Rhea had welcomed Jacob. Nicole would have him over two nights a week, leaving time for Haze and Gabby to be together and connect properly. The start of their relationship had been fraught with problems, and it was good to be able to get to know one another without all the drama. Nicole had come around to the idea of them being together. She still refrained from seeing Haze socially, but whenever Nicole came to pick up Jacob, some of their old banter came back. It was a slow process, but one Haze knew would be worth it in the end.

Gabby had been back at work for two months, leaving Haze to have Jacob through the day. Gabby had been hesitant at first, not wanting Haze to feel like a babysitter. Haze saw Jacob as her son too and was more than fine with the arrangement. She was able to spend time with him and work without issue. They had even looked into buying a bigger property, so Jacob could have his own room as he was still sharing with Haze and Gabby.

All in all, things were working out great. Haze had never been so happy. For so long she had been miserable, loving Gabby from afar. She never thought Gabby could love her back. The ring on her finger proved otherwise.

"I thought you were napping with us?" Gabby called from her place on the grass.

Haze looked up and grinned. "I was going to, but you both looked so peaceful I just had to draw you."

"Let me see."

Haze put down her pencil and stood. The drawing was nowhere near complete. She had only managed to get down the basic outline and contours of their faces before Gabby woke up. You could still see who it was. She went over to Gabby, bending down and kissing her lips. She sat next to her and held up her pad.

"Oh, Haze. It's beautiful."

"I've only just started."

Gabby tilted her head and kissed Haze's neck. "Your hands are really talented."

Haze's skin warmed over the double entendre. She put the pad down on the grass. "You're bad."

"You make me this way."

Haze turned serious. "I love you so much. Thank you for giving us a chance."

"I love you, too. And thank you for not giving up on me. I'm sorry it took so long for me to realise I love you."

Haze held up her hand, the sunlight glinting off her ring. "We have the rest of our lives together. It doesn't matter how long it took to get here." Jacob opened his eyes and smiled at Haze, who then scooped him up off the blanket and kissed his cheek.

"True, but thank you anyway."

Haze grinned at her. "No problem."

The End

ABOUT SAMANTHA HICKS

Samantha currently lives in the south west of England with her best buddy, Finley, her springer spaniel. She spends her time writing, drawing, and getting out into nature. Family and friends are the most important things to her, and she finds her inspiration for her stories from those closest to her. Writing has become her greatest passion, and after years of trying to find her confidence, shes finally decided to make a career out of it. She hopes to be doing this for the rest of her life. Sam has a thirst for reading, preferring it to almost anything, and she hopes, one day, to settle down by the beach.

OTHER AFFINITY BOOKS

One Shot at Love by Annette Mori
Blair returns to her hometown after the death of her sister. Always an activist she vows to use her voice to advocate for better gun control. She meets Maribel, an irresistible, sexy woman who proves to be an enigma to Blair. Maribel can't help approaching the weeping woman and learning the origin of Blair's grief, Maribel thinks she is the last person who should form a friendship with Blair. Ultimately, the allure is too much for Maribel, but how long can she keep her secret and continue to nurture their burgeoning feelings for one another. A committed left-wing social activist could never fall for the poster child of the NRA. Unless taking that one shot at love matters more than anything else.

The Mountain Whispers by Ali Spooner
Arriving home and discovering the betrayal by her best friend and lover, Eli Fortner leaves to run off her anger and

hurt. A chance stop at a convenience store and the purchase of lottery tickets sends Eli's life into a whirlwind of change. Able to now pursue her dreams, Eli heads off to see what else fate has in store for her.

Whit Brewer, Eli's neighbor, is everything Eli never knew she needed and wanted. But can she let go of the betrayal long enough to let Whit in? Thirteen black cats, a baby goat, and Cruz, her furry best friend, join Eli on her adventure, new life, and the possibility of real love.

Charlie by Erin O'Reilly

At fourteen, Hannah Garvin met 'the one,' Charlene Gaines, and her life was never the same. They were inseparable and spent every moment they could together. One day, Charlie left without a word and again, Hannah's life took a dramatic change. Hannah vowed to never fall in love again. When she meets Mick, a new arrival to the small Texas panhandle town near her family's farm, her heart remembers what being in love was like, and yearns for more. Will Hannah let the memory of Charlie go so she can start a new life with Mick? Or will her heart betray her and hold on to her love for Charlie?

Misha's Promise by Renee MacKenzie

Misha Wyatt has settled into a peaceful existence as a healer in Karst, New America. When an airplane crashes in the meadow outside of Karst, Misha hurries to help the pilot. Misha is not expecting the pilot to be alive...or so beautiful.

Will her uncontrollable desire to keep the pilot safe be her downfall? Can they survive their journey? The last book in the Karst series brings our characters to their physical and emotional limits. Don't miss the culmination of this exciting series!

Heart Strings Attached by Ali Spooner & Annette Mori
Socialite Remy has her world shaken. Bartender Chancy has her orderly life turned around. A mutually beneficial business agreement between Remy and Chancy turns into undeniable attraction. Will the two ignore culture norms to explore their intense desire for each other?

The Panty Thief by Annette Mori
Someone is stealing panties, but who? And why? Joey Hartford is a fourth-year medical student who insists she doesn't have time for a relationship. A new tenant in her apartment building is proving too tempting to ignore. Sabrina is in her final year of her doctoral program and focused on completing her dissertation. Meeting Joey is dangerous for so many reasons. Add a suicidal ex-girlfriend who suddenly reappears in Sabrina's life and Joey's jealous friend-with-benefits, and things get complicated quickly.

Country Living by Jen Silver
Peri Sanderson achieves her dream of moving from London to a cottage in the English countryside with her wife, Karla. Peri sees their future as pastoral while chatting with the

locals in a quaint village pub. Sexy urbanite, Karla, has other ideas. Secrets are everywhere. Peri quickly senses something not quite right among her rural neighbours and also with Karla. Temptation, betrayal, and intrigue combine to change the lives of both women beyond anything they could have imagined.

Before the Light by Samantha Hicks
One year after her long-time partner Meredith's abduction and their subsequent break-up, Kathleen Bowden-Scott's life is spiralling out of control. She meets Bethany Jones and despite an instant attraction Kathleen shies away. In this fast-paced, romantic suspense, lies are exposed and hearts unite as Kathleen and Beth fight for their future.

Wanted for Christmas by JM Dragon
Belle Farrow knew what she wanted for Christmas–work. She had little to offer but a minor degree in cookery and household management. Certainly not enough for a decent chef or housekeeper position. Then she saw an advert in the local newspaper. Wanted: Housekeeper/cook/nanny for the period of Christmas until the New Year. This is Christmas. Perhaps Santa reads the ad column too and pushes a little spirit of the season to that request.

Dreams in a Jar by JM Dragon
When you believe your life is a never-ending spiral of despair and the only personal joy you have is inside of a

novel, would you grab a chance to hide away in the local bookstore and dream of adventures? Thea's life is about to embark on a journey she never envisioned when local bookstore owner, Marion, is taken ill. Her niece, Sheryl Appleby, takes over the reins and her presence provides Thea the courage to take a leap of faith. Can she embrace the butterfly effect, or are Thea's dreams bottled in a jar forever?

Pleasure Workers by Annette Mori
Alex Cortez is accomplished at two things, fixing broken equipment and pleasuring women. She is happily doing both at the Ranch in Nevada. Danna Nichols, newly widowed, feels lost and alone. When her good friend Lindy invites her to check out the newly established Trophy Wives Club, it awakens dormant feelings and desires. An instant attraction happens and the two form a bond under unlikely circumstances. Will the challenges of their social status tear them apart before they can enjoy the pleasures of their new love?

The Trophy Wives Club by Ali Spooner
What happens when under-appreciated professional women are offered their dream jobs? When one of Atlanta's elite businesswomen and wife of a prominent judge sets her sights on a goal, life begins to change for these women. Friendships and romance bloom in a unique fitness club on the outskirts of Atlanta, where more than a workout is offered.

Unknown Forces by Samantha Hicks
Jennifer Wilson spent the last seventeen years raising her younger sister Kelsey after a boating accident killed their parents. Riley hasn't had an easy life either and her friendship with Kelsey is the only thing steadfast in her life. When tragedy and secrets emerge, Jennifer and Riley must learn to lean on each other. The growing attraction between them only complicates matters. When events conspire to keep them apart, will they trust the unknown forces that keep pushing them together, or hide from their feelings forever?

A Window to Love by Annette Mori
Two life events, two paths colliding, two souls destined to meet. Mandie Carter lives an uninspired life. No passion, no romance, and just when she thought things couldn't get worse, life throws her a curve. Gail Forrester is barely hanging on. Buried under mountains of debt, only her much in demand architectural designs keep her afloat. Now, they must find a way forward together through what life and destiny has in store for them. Only then can they hope to step into that window to love.

Affinity
Rainbow Publications

eBooks, Print, Free eBooks

Visit our website for more publications available online.

www.affinityrainbowpublications.com

Published by Affinity Rainbow Publications
A Division of Affinity eBook Press NZ LTD
Canterbury, New Zealand

Registered Company 2517228

www.ingramcontent.com/pod-product-compliance
Lightning Source LLC
Chambersburg PA
CBHW051646260626
47170CB00004B/1361